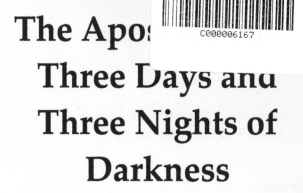

The Apos... Three Days and Three Nights of Darkness

Lindsay Hassall

GILEAD
B O O K S
PUBLISHING

First published in Great Britain, April 2022
www.GileadBooksPublishing.com

2 4 6 8 10 9 7 5 3 1

British Library Cataloguing-in-Publication Data:
A catalogue record for this book is available from
the British Library.

ISBN: 978-1-8381828-2-3

Cover design: Nathan Ward
Cover image: Adobestock/John Theodore

Introduction

In the Acts of the Apostles, we find the well-known true story of the man called Saul who was met by the Risen Lord, Jesus Christ, in a vision on the road to Damascus. This dramatic encounter changed him from being a persecutor of the church to becoming one of the foundation stones within the growth and development of the church. After the Gospels and the book of the Acts of the Apostles, we find that the majority of the remaining books in the New Testament comprise of the letters Paul himself wrote to the churches and to individuals to help guide and encourage them to grow in their faith and their service to their Lord, Jesus The Messiah.

The Acts of the Apostles tells us that Saul was blind for three days. We read the story and look back, but Saul was living in it. He did not know how long he was to be blinded for. He did not even know if he would ever regain his sight. Nor did he know how long he would have to wait before a stranger called Ananias was to visit him?

What did Saul think and pray during those few days? What happened to him? What comforted him in his blindness? What did the Pharisee of Pharisees have to face and confront to become one of those whom he was persecuting to prison and to death?

This book opens the door as to what could have happened when Saul finally arrives in the city of Damascus until he was visited by Ananias.

This book is perhaps the untold story of Saul.

> *My heart is overflowing with a good thought;*
> *I am speaking my works for the king;*
> *my tongue is the pen of a skilled scribe.*
> Psalm 45:1

Acts 9:1-18

Saul, still breathing out threats and murder against the disciples of the Lord, went to the high priest, and requested letters from him to the synagogues of Damascus, so that if he found any there of the Way, either men or women, he might bring them bound to Jerusalem. As he went he drew near Damascus, and suddenly a light from heaven shone around him. He fell to the ground and heard a voice saying to him, "Saul, Saul, why do you persecute Me?"

He said, "Who are You, Lord?"

The Lord said, "I am Jesus, whom you are persecuting. It is hard for you to kick against the goads." Trembling and astonished, he said, "Lord, what will You have me do?" The Lord said to him, "Rise up and go into the city, and you will be told what you must do."

The men traveling with him stood speechless, hearing the voice, but seeing no one. Saul rose up from the ground. And when his eyes were opened, he saw nothing. So they led him by the hand and brought him into Damascus. For three days he was without sight, and neither ate nor drank.

A disciple named Ananias was in Damascus. The Lord said to him in a vision, "Ananias."

He said, "Here I am, Lord."

The Lord said to him, "Rise and go to Straight Street, and inquire at Judas' house for someone named Saul of Tarsus, for he is praying, and has seen in a vision a man named Ananias coming in and putting his hand on him, so that he may see again."

Ananias answered, "Lord, I have heard from many about this man, how many evil things he has done to Your saints at Jerusalem. And here he has authority from the chief priests to bind all who call on Your name."

But the Lord said to him, "Go your way. For this man is a chosen vessel of Mine, to bear My name before the Gentiles and their kings, and before the sons of Israel. For I will show him how much he must suffer for My name's sake."

Then Ananias went his way and entered the house. Putting his hands on him, he said, "Brother Saul, *the Lord Jesus, who appeared to you on the way as you came, has sent me so that you may see again and be filled with the Holy Spirit." Immediately something like scales fell from his eyes, and he could see again. And he rose up and was baptized. When he had eaten, he was strengthened.*

A generation is several years. For our story it is 40.

Part one of our story takes place at the beginning of a generation. Three babies are born in different parts of the Roman Empire, but they all have things that unite them. They are born to God-fearing Jewish parents, they are boys, they are circumcised on the eighth day of their lives.

Part two of our story is located in time towards the end of that same generation.

Part One

To everything there is a season,
a time for every purpose under heaven:
a time to be born, and a time to die.
Ecclesiastes 3:1-2

Chapter One

There was no privacy. There was nowhere for the couple to hide. All those who were with them turned away their heads but continued to listen, wanting and waiting to help if needed. Those who had a god prayed for a safe birth, whilst others just wished and hoped. The servants' prison was no place for this young woman. She was there with her husband. Their first born was about to come into the world. Instead of their own family waiting nearby to rejoice with the new parents as the husband proudly held up their firstborn as would have happened in their homeland, in their Promised Land, in Israel, here they were in prison. No family surrounded them. Just a sea of unknown faces, other prisoners, like themselves from all over the Roman Empire. Slaves waiting to be sold and passed to their new owners. The husband had been praying in the days leading up to this precious moment, that he, his wife and their, soon to be, first born would remain together as a unit. They were not called a family here. They were a unit. They were now servants, slaves of Rome. He held on to the tassels of his prayer shawl hidden beneath his garments. 'Please, Lord, please Lord', he pleaded.

The baby, a boy was born. An elderly woman who did not speak the same language as the young woman assisted her as her son finally came into the world, into the prison, into slavery. Another thing Rome now owned. She slipped off her shawl and then shivered because of the damp cold air and wrapped the baby carefully and lovingly in it to keep him warm and then passed him to his mother. All the prisoners celebrated in their own way with what they could. They were all reminded of home, their own homes. A new life always brought hope. Hope of freedom. Hope of a future.

———————

'We must circumcise him,' the father said to the young mother. 'He needs to be part of our Covenant. It is his only hope.' They had been moved from the prison to the home of a rich Roman Officer in the Italian Regiment stationed within the city in Rome. The father's prayers had been answered. His family were still together. They were servants, or rather prisoners, until they could either earn their freedom or die. Slaves of all nationalities were here. The Officer was known for treating his slaves well compared to other owners, but they still had no rights, no freedom. They were slaves. They had no religion. They had no god. They were slaves. The father knew that to circumcise his child or indeed for any servant to sacrifice to their god was not acceptable and would be punished. Only the Roman gods ruled and reigned in this household. Only they could be worshipped. Despite this, the father had managed to arrange for an old Rabbi who lived nearby to come to the room his family shared with others. 'We must be quick,' the father had said. The Rabbi knew that he must not be caught in this house, but he had taken the risk to circumcise another one of God's chosen, precious children. He went through the ceremony as quickly as he could and left escorted by the father. Others watched but none would tell. They all had their secrets. They all wanted to remain alive. They all wanted to gain their freedom. Helping each other was their only way.

When they reached the street the father said, 'Rabbi. I have nothing to give you, to bless you with, to thank you for what you have done for us, for my son.' The father paused, 'Please keep these safe for me until we are free.' He handed the Rabbi a cloth which held his prayer shawl and a small golden Hannukah candlestick.' The father explained quickly that these were the only things of value that he and his wife had. They would not remain long in their possession in this household with the many searches. The Rabbi began to protest, 'How will you pray? How will you remember?' The father quickly explained that the hope of the servant-king, the Messiah would always burn bright in his heart. Their Messiah would come. Then they would be free. Free, to live and worship as God's chosen ones. And pray? The father had never stopped praying since they had lost their freedom. He constantly prayed for himself, his wife, and now he had his first-born son to live and to pray for.

As the Rabbi quickly hurried away into the darkness, he muttered to himself, 'I never asked the father and the mother for his name'. 'Oh well, you know it Lord.' The Rabbi prayed, 'Keep your hand upon him and bless him. He will need it.' The Rabbi continued to pray for the boy he had just circumcised as he went through the dark streets and made his way back to his home holding tight to the Prayer Shawl through which he could feel to shape of the candlestick.

Chapter Two

The luxurious home of the Rabbi was full to overflowing with people. Family, friends, physicians, servants, all mingled together. The Rabbi's wife was about to give birth to his first born. He was hoping for a son who would follow in his footsteps. He imagined the future and then the cries of his wife in her last few hours of labour brought him back to the present.

The Rabbi held up his son for all to see. He was so proud, so grateful. His son would never want for anything. He passed his first born back to his mother who tenderly and lovingly caressed him, held him, fed him. She was pleased that she had presented her husband with not just a healthy first-born child but a son at that. She hoped that a daughter for her would come later.

The Rabbi's home was full once again. This time for the circumcision of his first born. He was a wealthy Rabbi who owned a Roman Villa and so had the space to welcome many friends and family to his home. A visiting Rabbi from Jerusalem had been invited along with the local Rabbi to perform this wonderful auspicious ceremony. No expense had been spared. The moment came. 'His Name?' Rabbi Gamaliel, who was part of the Sanhedrin, asked. 'Saul', his father proudly announced.

Chapter Three

The Levitical shepherds saw the man with his wife. They helped her into the birthing tower. 'Is this allowed?' one of them asked. 'This is only for the Temple lambs. What will the authorities say?' 'This is our secret. No-one need know,' replied one of the older ones. The shepherds left the, soon to be, father and mother, and returned to their sheep. The birthing room was no place for them tonight. Ewes and lambs, yes. Mothers and babies, well that was another matter.

The husband was a righteous man, loving and caring. His wife was special to him. He held her hand and whispered, 'Mary, God is with us. All will be well.' Somehow, he and Mary just knew what to do that night. Their first-born son was born. They both took turns admiring him, kissing him, thanking God for him, and then they wrapped him in swaddling clothes and laid him in the manger to sleep. The manger, the place where the new-born lambs were laid. The lambs laid in these mangers were born to die for they were destined for the altar in the Temple. Lambs were needed all the year round in the worship of God. The lambs were wrapped in swaddling clothes and laid in the manger for safety so that they remained perfect, unblemished and unbruised. Many lambs were needed at Passover but as this was Tabernacles things were quieter for the shepherds and the birthing tower for the ewes was not in use all the time. This night the manger cradled not a lamb destined for the altar but a child, a boy, a son, Mary's son.

The father and mother had been moved from the birthing tower escorted by the shepherds to a nearby home. The father helped the mother, whilst the Shepherds carried the baby with such pride and tenderness. It was as if he was theirs, one of their own. The family were welcomed into the home and were treated as royalty. They knew in this part of the country who the father was, his genealogy, who he was descended from.

The father, when the day came for his son to be circumcised, went with one of the shepherds to fetch the Rabbi. Mary held her son close to her. She knew this was God's way, this was a sign of his covenant, but this was her precious son, and she couldn't bear to think of him being hurt, cut or bruised. She passed him to his father who passed him to the Rabbi. Mary smiled through her tears as she could see the tenderness and love in the Rabbi's eyes as he held her son. Did he know what they knew? Had the angel appeared to him also? 'What is his name?' the Rabbi asked the father. Mary quickly whispered 'Jesus' and the father smiled in agreement. 'Of course,' the Rabbi said. 'Please don't hurt him,' she prayed under her breath. The elderly Rabbi continued with the ritual established by Abraham, their father in the faith. But then he paused. He looked up as if he was listening and then with moist eyes looked at the mother and said, quoting from one of the ancient prophets:

> *Therefore the Lord Himself shall give you a sign: The virgin shall conceive, and bear a son, and shall call his name Immanuel.*
> Isaiah 7:14

Part Two

Chapter Four

Stephen, the first Christian martyr, had been buried. The witnesses against Stephen, the first people by Law called upon to cast the first stones, had laid their garments at the feet of a young Rabbi called Saul. This young Rabbi is now present at the meeting of the Sanhedrin in the City of Jerusalem.

The Rabbi stood waiting. He was leaning against the wall of the vestibule which led into the Sanhedrin Court. He was sweating, not because of heat due to being in the city during the summer months, but because of nerves, excitement, anticipation, adrenaline. He had been given a few minutes to make his speech to the court and then he was asked to step outside.

He felt that he was so privileged and honoured to be here, to have been interviewed by the Sanhedrin. He was quietly praying to God that he would be the chosen one. He had always been eager to serve his people, his nation, and his God, but he had never expected that he would find himself here, within the Sanhedrin Court addressing them.

The Rabbi had devoted himself from an early age to studying the Torah. He had advanced far beyond his years in the faith and in his learning thanks to many people. One person he was so thankful to was his father who was also a Pharisee. It was his father who had inspired him to seek the jewels and riches buried deep within God's Holy Word. The Rabbi had always loved and respected his father and wanted to follow in his footsteps. He wanted to be like him. He was also grateful to his mother. He didn't want to disappoint her, and she was one of the reasons he had studied so hard. He loved her and cherished her praises. Not only had she supported him, but she had also quietly and secretly studied so she could discuss and debate at home with both her husband and her son. The husband she loved and the son she was so proud of.

The Rabbi waited. 'How much longer?' he muttered. Patience had never been one of his virtues. Some of the people in Council knew him. He was confident that he had their support and that they would vote for him. Others had heard of him but had never met him. These were the people who had needed to be convinced that he could be the one. They had been expecting to appoint an older man to the task, but they were impressed by his zeal and the promise he showed. The Rabbi was praying that he would gain their votes.

These leaders of the nation of Israel had a vision, a dream. God's mighty Kingdom to be established on earth. Israel, God's chosen nation, his chosen people, to be restored to their rightful place of glory on the world's stage once more. For this to happen they had to remove the apostasy that was spreading. To purify the Land. To keep the faith pure. To protect the people of Israel from the deceptions and heresies that were spreading. The blasphemers and their followers needed exposing so that God's elect would be protected from going astray in these last days. There were many pretend Messiahs and false prophets amongst the people and this Jesus was just another one of them. He was dead and it was now his followers who needed removing from the nation for they were the yeast, the sin, that was polluting what was chosen and called by God to be holy and pure. The Rabbi quoted to himself:

> *For the lips of an immoral woman drip as a honeycomb,*
>   *and her mouth is smoother than oil.*
> *But her end is bitter as wormwood,*
>   *sharp as a two-edged sword.*
> *Her feet go down to death,*
>   *her steps take hold of Sheol.*
> Proverbs 5:3-35

The Rabbi had taught that the immoral woman was heresy and those who embraced her would end up in

Sheol. All who followed Jesus would also end up in Sheol. They were all on a slippery road that they would be unable to return from. This teaching was one of things that had attracted the attention of the Sanhedrin to him. He prayed that he would be the one chosen to bring salvation to the nation.

When Israel had entered the Promised Land, God forbade the nation from mixing with the inhabitants of the Land. They were commanded to remove them, otherwise they would be led astray by their false gods. History was now repeating itself. Israel was being led astray again but this time from within the nation by the misguided and gullible few. The evil, the sin, the yeast, needed removing before the whole nation was affected and brought under the judgement of God. If Israel would repent, turn to God and seek his face, then he would send the Messiah. The Kingdom would then be established, God's Kingdom would be seen and manifested on earth.

The Rabbi quickly turned as the door to the court room was opened. He was ushered back inside. He knew that the discussion was over. They had voted. Their decision was made, but what was it? The atmosphere, their faces, gave nothing away. Finally, after a few preliminary pleasantries, the Chief Priest spoke. The Rabbi was asked to step forward. The Chief Priest explained to the Rabbi that the prophet, Jesus from Nazareth in Galilee, had been tried and found guilty of blasphemy. Jesus had spoken about himself being the Messiah, declaring himself equal with the Almighty. The Rabbi needed to ensure that this nonsense about Jesus was purged from the Land. The Land must be cleansed from such heresy. His name and his movement must be eliminated from amongst God's children. His supporters and his followers must be silenced. Such people were putting the land and the nation in a place of great danger, not just with the Roman Government but, more importantly, with God himself. The Rabbi had the vote of the Council. He was to be the one who on behalf of the Sanhedrin would bring healing and restoration to the nation.

The Court was dismissed by the Chief Rabbi. The assembly dispersed. Its members gathered together in their select groups whilst the Rabbi waited patiently until the scribes gave to him letters of authority. In amongst these letters would be the documents that would enable him to obtain the necessary Temple funds and personnel to help him.

The Rabbi himself, in his teaching and preaching, had often entreated Israel to repent, turn to God and seek his face again. If only Israel would uphold the Law, then God would send the Messiah. The Kingdom of God and Israel would be established this time for a thousand years. Now he, a Rabbi and a Pharisee, could usher in the Messiah.

The Rabbi left the court a proud man, a chosen man, a man with a divine mission, a man with a purpose, a man full of zeal.

As he left the Temple precincts and passed through the city, he was thinking about his task and planning the next few weeks. He would conclude this, his first trip, at Damascus. He was determined to visit as many synagogues as possible along the way, making arrests of all the followers of this false Messiah. However, he was distracted from his planning by the thought of how to write and share all of this with his sister. She would be waiting to hear from him. She would be so proud of him as his mother would have been had she still been alive. His younger sister was always proud of his successes and achievements. His advancement in the study of the Torah, his appointment as a Rabbi, his acceptance into the elite holiness movement of the Pharisees. And now he was the one chosen to purify the Land, the Promised Land of Israel, from apostasy and to restore her to a place of honour in the world and to help prepare the way for the coming Messiah. He was full of zeal. It overflowed from him to everyone he talked to about his mission. The Rabbi was pursuing his task with such fervour that some of his friends had joked that this was really his mission and that he had managed to arrange for the Sanhedrin to not only approve it but also fund it. The Rabbi ignored their taunts. They were jealous of what he would become through this task that lay before him and the success that would be his and his alone.

The Rabbi vowed to himself using the words of Psalm 132:

> *I will not come into my house,*
> *nor go up to my bed;*
> *I will not give sleep to my eyes,*
> *or slumber to my eyelids,*
> *until I find a place for the Lord,*
> *a dwelling for the mighty God of Jacob.*
> Psalm 132: 3-5

Later that day in the quiet of his room he began to write to his sister. He found it difficult to contain his excitement as he quickly wrote and shared with her his thoughts and plans.

Chapter Five

The Rabbi had made arrangements to finish his first trip at the House of Judas in Damascus and had sent word ahead to prepare for his arrival.

J udas had many reasons to look forward to the Rabbi's visit. They were close friends. They had studied together. Judas respected the Rabbi for his reverence and the honour in which he held the Covenant, the Faith, the Law and the Prophets. The Rabbi was a Pharisee, something which Judas envied him for, as he himself also aspired to attain to that same level of holiness and devotion in his life. Judas also desired to see God's chosen people sanctified and preserved. He whole heartedly supported the government and the mission the Rabbi was leading. Judas wanted revival amongst God's people. He was waiting for the reestablishment of Israel's golden age. He was expecting God's Kingdom to be established on the earth and especially in Israel. *The prophecies, the prophecies will soon be fulfilled* he thought to himself. He was eagerly waiting for his friend to arrive.

The House of Judas was prepared for the arrival of the Rabbi whose reputation was travelling faster than he was. It was just after noon and the Rabbi was expected shortly. Travelling with him and his companions were the Temple Police assigned to him by the Captain of the Temple Guard under the authority of the High Priest. News of their impending arrival rippled through the servant's quarters who referred to the Police as being more like thugs from the backstreets rather than Temple employees. Judas had assigned one of his most trusted servants to attend to the Rabbi when he arrived.

The Rabbi's journey had already taken several weeks from Jerusalem and his quarters had been carefully prepared. Judas had placed in his room some of the latest scrolls from the Synagogue Torah School for his friend to read and review for him. He and his guests would need to refresh themselves and rest before they completed their mission in Damascus, but Judas knew that the Rabbi always found time to read, study and debate at the table no matter how busy he was with his duties. The Rabbi in his letter had confided in Judas that after their return to the Holy City they would prepare for another trip, this time towards the south of the country.

Rumours were rife amongst the servants. Despite whatever the Government in Jerusalem was saying, the word amongst the servants and in the marketplace was that the Rabbi was leading an ethnic cleansing program which sounded absurd. This was the kind of thing the Gentiles did. Some called it a necessary religious reform movement. Whatever it was called, many were in fear in case they were wrongly arrested, for the Rabbi was not known for his leniency. He was accusing people of blasphemy just for mentioning the name of Jesus in his presence. Furthermore, it was said that some of the synagogue leaders had assisted him by providing the names of not just believers but also known troublemakers who had nothing to do with Jesus. Many leaders saw this as an opportunity to remove from the society and cleanse the Land of both unbelievers and troublemakers.

A few years before, Jesus had been condemned to death for blasphemy. Many had believed in the stories of an empty grave, that he had been raised up, that he had not just been seen but also embraced by his followers. The word about him was always spreading, always being spoken about. But now there was this young overzealous Rabbi. No longer could you be just thrown out of the synagogue as happened when Jesus was alive, but now it was imprisonment and death for believing Jesus was the Messiah and that he had been raised from the dead. This Rabbi was a persecutor with the full backing and authority of the High Priests and the Sanhedrin. Many feared what would happen if he was not stopped. Would he arrest all of Israel? King Solomon in his Song of Songs had warned about the little foxes in the vineyard. This was not just a little fox, but a fully-grown, rabid fox deliberately let loose. His zeal was not just expressed with a passion at the table in discussion or in the synagogue with debate, but in the streets with his thugs, licensed thugs.

Many said that this Rabbi was doing what the Roman armies had tried and failed to do ever since they had invaded the country. They had sought to weaken the nation and strip it of its religion which was a uniting factor amongst them, to make unity amongst the Jews a thing of the past. The Rabbi was causing polarisation, division in the Land between those who believed that Jesus was the Messiah and those who did not. The Rabbi was a part of that Israel that did not believe. The servant assigned to Judas was a part of the Israel that did believe. He was not looking forward to the Rabbi's visit.

The servant sighed heavily as he rechecked the room assigned to the Rabbi. Persecution was at his heels once again. He had believed he was safe in Damascus. He had had the opportunity of visiting Jerusalem with Judas and his household for many of the festivals. But, in the privacy and the quiet of his room each year he had lit the small golden Hannukah candlestick given to him by his father and silently remembered before God how his family had been rescued and saved from slavery in Rome. They were now safe in Damascus and had been for many years. His father's crime in Rome was being Jewish. A pagan merchant wanted revenge on the Jewish business manager who was shrewder than he was. The servant knew his father was wise and shrewd, but he was also honest and fair, unlike the merchant. A false accusation with false witnesses, before his father could defend himself, he was condemned to be a servant.

The servant thought about his childhood in Rome. His father after seven long years as a slave was able to gain his freedom and keep his wife and son with him. Then he was a young boy but not too young to not know about the fear, the restrictions within the soldier's house. They established a life together in the outskirts of Rome. It was not easy for his parents, but they were free and still together. Rome then, unofficially of course, began to force Jews out of the city. So, his father, fearing slavery again or imprisonment, left the vicinity of Rome and came to Damascus. Jews were safe in Damascus.

They had received a lot of help along the way from the various synagogues they visited. Their people were always hospitable to their own. Once they had arrived in Damascus his father had found work. Before he had been enslaved, he had been a skilled administrator and manager for several merchants. When his son had been old enough to work, his father had gained for him this position working in the house of Judas, the home of one of the synagogue leaders. To the servant it was like the home with his parents. A place of safety, a place of refuge. A place where God was honoured and a place where he could forget Rome. He was happy and enjoyed serving his master, Judas. Now that the Rabbi was coming to persecute the followers of Jesus, he was not so sure he was in such a place of refuge and safety after all. His family had fled Rome because they were Jewish. Now he was afraid that he would have to flee again, this time because of his faith in the Jewish Messiah. He feared for his safety. He feared for his parents. He feared he would have to leave this household, this city and find somewhere else to live. He longed for a place of freedom and peace.

Chapter Six

In Damascus lived a devout man according to the Law of Moses, a man called Ananias. He was also a believer in Jesus as the Messiah.

Ananias moved around his home. He had been blessed in his long years and had prospered. He lived in the city in a large, spacious house located near to the synagogue he attended. He enjoyed the courtyard in the centre of his home. It boasted a fountain and a small garden. It enabled him to meditate and to pray. It was also the place where the followers of Jesus in the city would regularly gather. His usually quiet home was now heaving with people. Since the death of Stephen in

Jerusalem many saints from the church had fled from there. When it was known that Ananias was willing to open up his home to the fleeing refugees several families had been sent into his care by the apostles. He had welcomed all who had arrived and promised shelter for them as long as he could. As he walked around the courtyard the children were playing in the fountain. He smiled and thanked God that he was wealthy and was able to provide all that these saints needed. Damascus was a quiet place for them. The religious leaders of Damascus, although at first against the movement that had begun with Jesus, did not believe persecution was necessary nor the answer to the problem. They were supporters of Gamaliel, his teachings and his views. Gamaliel was known for his wisdom. It was now common knowledge about how he had spoken to the Sanhedrin when Peter and the other apostles were arrested. He had said:

Now I tell you, keep away from these men and leave them alone, because if this intention or this activity is of men, it will come to nothing. But if it is of God, you will not be able to overthrow them, lest perhaps you be found even fighting against God.

Acts 5:38-40

If the truth were known the city had changed its policy from tolerating the followers of Jesus to welcoming them primarily because of Ananias. He was held in high esteem by many Jews in the city and they all spoke well of him. He and the other followers of Jesus had shown by their love and their lives that they were devout according to the law, in fact, probably more devout than many who opposed the movement and called them the blasphemers. But persecution was now on its way. Why? Had the city leaders shifted their position? Had they reversed their policy? But, when? And why?

Ananias walked around his garden smelling the different herbs. He was meditating on the words of Jesus and was thinking what to share with the saints. He needed direction as to how to care and look after his growing flock. They were afraid of what might happen when the persecutor arrived. This was the reason they had left Jerusalem and fled from their homes and their businesses. Jesus had spoken about it:

> So when you see the 'abomination of desolation,' spoken of by Daniel the prophet, then let those who are in Judea flee to the mountains. Let him who is on the housetop not go down to take anything out of his house. Let him who is in the field not return to take his clothes. Woe to those who are with child and to those who nurse in those days! Pray that your escape will not be in the winter or on the Sabbath. For then will be great tribulation, such as has not happened since the beginning of the world until now, no, nor ever shall be.
>
> Matthew 24:15-21

Is this what Daniel had been prophesying? Is this what Jesus was referring to? This Rabbi has been standing in the Temple and he was the one causing the saints to flee. Was he bringing in the tribulation? Was he the abomination of desolation?

Chapter Seven

The Rabbi had visited many villages since he had left Jerusalem. He had made numerous arrests. His mission was successful. He was in high spirits. Damascus was not far away. He could see it in the distance. The Rabbi was looking forward to a few days of rest with his dear friend Judas before purging the name of Jesus from the city. Perhaps Judas would invite him to speak in his synagogue.

The Rabbi was laughing and taunting his travelling companions. 'Come on, race, run!' he kept yelling at them. They wondered how the Rabbi could be so fit. He was small and muscular but surprisingly very fast on his feet and also nimble.

They had expected him to slow down but he had kept up a steady fast pace for over two miles. They were exhausted and had to stop whilst the Rabbi, stopping with them, was just laughing at how unfit they were. They did not know that he was a citizen of both Rome and Israel and when he had been growing up had taken full advantage of both citizenships. The Romans worshiped their bodies and were proud of their fitness. The Israelites worshiped their God and were proud of their Torah. So, he joined in at the gym and found the training exhilarating and refreshing after the many long hours of Torah study. He had lived a double life and that was one of his skills, why he had survived. He could throw himself into what lay before him without compromising his faith and his love for God. His parents were concerned at first but then realised that God must have his hand upon their son as he shared with them his victories in the gym alongside his encounters with God through his prayers and study times. As he was growing up none of his peers in the gym were really bothered that he was a Jew and those that did soon regretted it when

44

they faced him in the boxing ring. He was a formidable opponent, refusing to give up even when he could hardly stand. He had also proved to be a match for many of the wrestlers and runners. As he grew into a promising athlete he also grew in piety, righteousness and in the knowledge of the Torah and the wisdom of his forefathers. As he laughed and joked with his exhausted travelling companions, he thought can life get any better this. His mission was proving successful. The results were impressive. Life was so good. His God was so good to him.

As he went he drew near Damascus, and suddenly a light from heaven shone around him. He fell to the ground and heard a voice saying to him, "Saul, Saul, why do you persecute Me?" The men traveling with him stood speechless, hearing the voice, but seeing no one. Saul rose up from the ground. And when his eyes were opened, he saw nothing. So they led him by the hand and brought him into Damascus. For three

days he was without sight, and neither ate nor
drank.

Acts 9:3-4,7-9

There was panic. There was fear. The Rabbi's
travelling companions were unsure of what to do.
They were bemused. They watched the Rabbi stand
on his feet, look up, put his hands to his eyes, and then
drop to his knees and look up as if he was begging,
pleading with someone or something unseen. Tears
were in his eyes. No one moved. Even their donkeys
were still. After what seemed an age, which was in
fact only a few minutes, the Rabbi, stood up and
stared. His eyes were lifeless.

The Rabbi was unable to see. Was he blind?

One by one the travelling companions took hold of
their donkeys and slowly moved together to
continue. No one spoke. They did not communicate
with each other than to glance at one another to see
what the other was doing. Someone approached the

Rabbi. They took him by the hand as they would have done a small child who was lost and needed to be taken home to its parents. The group moved along silently. From the Rabbi's lifeless eyes, tears were flowing. His companions wanted to know what had happened, but no one dared speak let alone address the Rabbi and he remained stunned, in total silence.

They were not far from the city. The party naturally divided. Again, no orders were given, no words were spoken. Some went on ahead into Damascus as the city gates came into view, whilst the remainder stayed with the Rabbi.

The Rabbi slowly entered the city. His appearing at the gates did not arouse any interest from the traders or those purchasing their wares. Children ran to and fro. Life was normal here, so the Rabbi's companions began to raise their heads and speak with one another. This they could understand, the hustle and bustle of life in a city, so they felt confident to engage with each other again. What happened on the road? That was a mystery. Beyond words. Beyond understanding. They led the Rabbi, who had still not spoken, to Straight Street where Judas's house was.

The travellers had missed the midday meal, but Judas had ensured that there was food for them all. Judas welcomed and embraced his friend. The Rabbi returned the embrace but said nothing, shared nothing, revealed nothing. Judas had heard whispers about the event on the road from those who had arrived first and he was expecting to learn more from his friend, but his friend was silent. It was as if he had been struck dumb as well as blind. Judas wondered what had happened on the road to his home. *What had happened to his friend*?

The Rabbi remained in his room the remainder of the afternoon. He needed solitude. He lay on the bed, fully clothed, with his prayer shawl around him. It was warm but the Rabbi was shivering. Not from the cold but from the experience. It was as if something had touched him inside so deeply that something within him had died. He felt inside as if he was weeping. Weeping for something he had lost.

The Rabbi closed his eyes to momentarily escape. To escape from his blindness. To escape from the world. He needed to think. He needed to pray.

The servant quietly opened the door and put a small pitcher of water and a cup on the table next to the Rabbi. He told the Rabbi he was outside, waiting, listening, in case the Rabbi needed him. He wondered if the Rabbi was asleep as there was no response, no acknowledgment from him at all. The servant then quietly shut the door and waited.

The servant began to reflect on all that had happened in the last few hours. Some of the Rabbi's party had arrived. They were...well...when they began their story it was thought that the party had been ambushed as they had neared the city and the Rabbi had been killed. Then the Rabbi had arrived. Being led by the hand like a little child. He was blind. He was silent. Judas had barked out orders. His concern was for his friend, the Rabbi. He must be cared for. The physicians must be called for. And then more of the story came out. Judas had listened to each person. Could what they have described be the appearing of the Glory of God? Some said they had heard thunder, others a voice but when he questioned them, he could not discover what the voice had said. It was as if they too were too stunned to talk about the incident clearly. Once the Rabbi had been escorted to his room Judas had spoken to all of the household. The Rabbi must be looked after and cared for he told them.

When the late comers had eaten and retired to rest, the servant heard his master Judas approaching and he arose from his seat out of respect for his master. Judas nodded to acknowledge him and after finding out from him that the Rabbi had not called for him, he quietly entered the room to be with his friend. The servant shut the door behind Judas and heard the soft tones of his master talking with his friend. It was obvious that Judas cared very much for the Rabbi. The servant then heard the Rabbi's voice. It was broken. It was like someone...bereaved? This was not the voice of the Rabbi that they had all come to know from his previous visits to Damascus. Judas opened the door and walked past the servant not acknowledging him this time. As he passed, the servant noticed concern and confusion on Judas's face.

What am I going to do with my friend? What has happened to him? These questions were causing Judas much pain and heartache.

Once the Rabbi was alone again, he lay back, holding back the tears.

After several hours the Rabbi sat up and swung his legs over the edge of the bed, placed his feet on the ground and his head into his hands. The Rabbi wept. 'I can't live like this!' He stood up and raised his head.

He was angry, at whom or what about he didn't know. He was also frustrated, at what or about what he didn't know. Whatever these emotions were, they were overwhelming him. They suddenly exploded within him and he lashed out as if he was attacking something or someone. He could feel the sun's warmth on his face and hit out into his darkness. He hated the sun. He hated the darkness even more. He hated his emotions. He hated life!

In his anger all he achieved was to kick over the table which caused the small pitcher of water to fall to the marble floor and smash. He fell on his knees amidst the spilt water and broken pottery and then onto his face and wept, and moaned, and begged and pleaded. The words of Jesus. He couldn't get them out of his head.

The servant heard the commotion from within but stood, listening, waiting.

Lying there the Rabbi remembered how with pride he had left the Sanhedrin. When the time came to leave Jerusalem and begin his mission, he had been breathing murder, wanting to hurt and to kill. But why? The Rabbi couldn't understand why he was so full of anger and hate. It was consuming him.

He knew these people were misled and needed punishing but what he was doing was beyond human reasoning. It was as if he was carrying out a personal vendetta.

The Rabbi sobbed in prayer, 'I do not understand why I am like this?' 'I don't want to be who I am. I despise what I have become.'

He was a Pharisee. He was one of the few people who were faithful and righteous according to the Covenant. He was honoured and praised because of this. He was honoured in society; he was privileged in the synagogues. He was passionately in love with the Torah and his God. But he now realised that there was a side of him that he didn't like.

'Lord, help me,' he pleaded.

The Rabbi felt the fear of living in darkness, of not being able to see whether it was day or night, of not being in control. The Rabbi also felt the fear of suddenly being alone, alone without God. When he normally prayed, he felt peace, the peace that comes from being close to God, in his presence, but now in his prayers he felt alone, in spiritual darkness. On the road, in the vision he knew he was in the presence of the Holy One of Israel. He knew he was in the presence of the Divine. But now he felt rejected. He felt as if God had abandoned him. Why had God turned his back on him? Why didn't God help him in his affliction? He felt reproach. He felt shame.

'Lord, help me,' He cried.

The Rabbi prayed:

> *Hear my cry, O God,*
> *attend to my prayer.*
> *From the end of the earth I will cry to You;*
> *when my heart faints,*
> *lead me to the rock that is higher than I.*
> *For You have been a refuge for me,*
> *and a strong tower from the enemy.*
> *I will abide in Your tent forever;*
> *I will seek refuge in the covering of Your wings.*
> Psalm 61:1-4

Chapter Eight

The First Night of darkness.

The servant listened at the door trying to discern what was happening within. The Rabbi was quiet. The servant hesitated and then after hearing nothing, he gently knocked at the door. Nothing, so he quietly opened the door and saw the Rabbi sitting on the bed with his feet amidst the broken pottery and spilled water. The Rabbi turned his head to look at him. It was a natural habit with the Rabbi, to look at the person who had entered. The old habit took over even though he was blind. The servant quietly said, 'May I help Rabbi and clean up for you?' The Rabbi thanked him and apologised for the accident. He lay back on the bed so as not to be a further hindrance to the servant. No more words were spoken. The servant cleared up the broken pottery and returned a few minutes later with another jar of water and cup, with cloths to dry the floor and table.

The Rabbi lay on the bed feeling ashamed of what he had done. The servant withdrew feeling foolish that he had just lit the lamp to light the room for a blind man.

The Rabbi lay back allowing his body to relax now he was alone again. Holding his prayer shawl tightly around him he quietly prayed. He began with the Psalms. He had prayed one of the Psalms each day for several years in his own private prayer times. These were separate from the set times of prayer he also faithfully and diligently followed. The Psalms were so familiar to him, like old friends. They were his security. They helped him focus on God. They were his rock in times of trouble. After reciting the Psalm, he prayed,

'Lord, I need help'.

'What is happening to me?
Please set my feet upon the rock.
Lord, help me, minister to me.
Lord, I repent of the things which upon reflection I did not handle well.
I need help.
I need compassion and mercy to be shown to me by you.'

He then paused and bowed his head. After several minutes he continued,

'Lord, I come to meet with you, to seek your face.
I need you.
You are my God.
You are my creator.
You are my rock.

You are my hiding place.

You are my strong tower.

I place myself into your hands.

Do not hide your face from me.

Do not hide yourself from me.'

The Rabbi in the stillness of the night thought about the journey and the road.

The light. It was so bright that everything else had disappeared. It suddenly appeared like lightening from Heaven but did not disappear as lightning does but remained. It was more dazzling than the sun at midday in summer with no clouds to hide it. He remembered how intensely white the light was. It was painful to look at, but it was also hard to turn away from. In fact, he couldn't turn away because it enveloped him, it was all around him. It wasn't shining from one source, like the sun. It was everywhere. Its source was all around him. He was in the light with no escape, no relief from its glare.

He also remembered the heaviness. The light was so heavy that he could not stand. He had not knelt of his own accord. It was as if he had to kneel. His legs could not hold him because of the weight of the light. The light had forced him to his knees.

He wondered if he had been transported to heaven. Nothing existed but that light. It was so intense. It also carried a warmth. It was like warm liquid love flowing through him and over him. In the light he had felt so accepted, so loved. He had never felt so close to God before. He wondered if he had stretched out his hand would he have touched him!

And there was also the awe. He knew he was in the presence of holiness. The presence, the power, the intensity. It was as if he was being consumed.

But when the voice spoke, he felt judged. Every cell in his body shook and trembled. That voice. It boomed with an authority he had never experienced before. It was as if he was in the voice, as every cell of his being heard the voice. The voice had spoken to him. He didn't have to try and recall what the voice had said. Those words had been burned into his heart and mind. He would never ever forget them. Not just the voice and the love within that voice but also the sorrow, the pain that was mixed with the love.

The Rabbi had felt as if nothing else existed except the light and himself. Everything else had faded away or disappeared.

Once the words were spoken there was the silence, stillness, such peace. The Rabbi did not know how long the peace lasted. The light was still shining and engulfing him. To him time had ceased to exist. He was in eternity. Then he felt that whatever realm he was in, whatever place he had visited, he was leaving it and returning to the road.

The Rabbi knew he had heard the voice of the Lord and wanted to obey whatever was asked of him. To the Rabbi there was no choice. His desire, his will was to obey whatever the Lord had told him to do. Anything he had ever read in the Torah he wanted to build into his life. To obey God's commands, to hear and obey his voice was the Rabbi's purpose for living and breathing.

The Rabbi remembered what he had heard:

"Saul, Saul, why do you persecute Me?"

"I am Jesus, whom you are persecuting. It is hard for you to kick against the goads."

"Rise up and go into the city, and you will be told what you must do."

He began to pray and meditate on what the Lord had said to him, wondering what he would be asked to do.

The Rabbi in his wondering had allowed his mind to wander...to dream...but then, it was if he was jerked back to reality. He said, 'But Jesus, you are dead!'

The Rabbi continued,

'Jesus, you were crucified. How is it that you are alive?'

'I don't understand.'

The Rabbi was tormented by what Jesus had said:

"Saul, Saul, why do you persecute Me?"

"I am Jesus, whom you are persecuting."

The Rabbi lay quietly on the bed. Sleep eluded him. His body was tired and needed to stretch out, to rest, but his mind was active, racing with thoughts. He was realising that the Lord whom he loved and wanted to serve, had revealed himself as Jesus! Jesus had said that persecuting his followers was persecuting him.

So many questions. The Rabbi had so many questions. The Lord had met with him. This was something he had always dreamed of and desired for, to meet the Lord. Moses had met the Lord at the Burning Bush. The prophets had heard the voice of the Lord. Some had even seen Him in visions. It was Isaiah who had said:

> *I clearly saw the Lord. He was seated on His exalted throne, towering high above me.*
> Isaiah 6:1

But when the Lord had appeared to him, it was Jesus. His Lord was Jesus?

The Rabbi began to think as the scholar again. He knew the prophecies about the Messiah and Jesus did not fulfil any of them. To begin with he was not born in Bethlehem but heralded from the North, from the Galilee region. Nazareth or Capernaum. To prove Jesus could not be the Messiah, in the quietness, in the darkness, the Rabbi started quietly reciting to himself the Psalms and the prophecies he knew so well about the Messiah. After several hours his trained mind confirmed that these scriptures did not refer to Jesus, but his heart was raising doubts within him, questioning his scholarly teaching and logic. His mind was saying, no! But his spirit was saying something different...could it be, yes?

Hours passed. The servant was outside waiting, listening. He knew the Rabbi was not asleep. He was praying, talking, reciting, arguing. He could tell by his chants, the change in his tone but he was unable to hear all the words. They were muffled not just by the door but by the tears, the weeping, the groanings.

The Rabbi struggled with his thoughts. The scriptures taught that the coming Messiah was to be a warrior, a King. One who brings redemption to the nation that is in bondage to a gentile empire. This was the kind of Messiah the Rabbi believed in, hoped for, looked for. But how could this Jesus be the Messiah? He was no King. He was no warrior. He had suffered and died and had died a cursed death at that. No Messiah would die such a cursed death. The Rabbi shook his head. 'None of this makes any sense.'

The Rabbi then quoted to himself one of the Psalms:

> *Lift up your heads, O you gates;*
> > *and be lifted up, you everlasting doors,*
> > *that the King of glory may enter.*
> *Who is this King of glory?*
> > *The Lord strong and mighty,*
> > *The Lord mighty in battle.*
> *Lift up your heads, O you gates;*
> > *lift up, you everlasting doors,*
> > *that the King of glory may enter.*
> *Who is He—this King of glory?*
> > *The Lord of Hosts,*

He is the King of glory

Psalm 24:7-10

The Rabbi said,

'The King of the Glory, he is the Messiah.

The Messiah is strong, he is mighty.

The Messiah is the leader of the armies of heaven.

The Messiah is to bring back to Israel all that has been lost.

He is to bring in the Glory of God.

He is to bring in God's Kingdom.'

He pulled his prayer shawl tighter as if he wanted to shut out the world and silence the questions. He wanted to lose himself in his prayer tent and lose himself in his rock, in his hiding place, in his God, in the one he knew and could trust. The one he could understand.

After a few minutes the Rabbi shrugged his shoulders and said, 'Jesus, if you are the Messiah, the King of Glory, why did you die?'

In his darkness, in his questioning, in his praying he was trying to reconcile himself to a new life, a life of blindness. It was a life he feared because he was a Torah scholar. How could he study without reading? How could he read and study God's Word? The thought of a life without scrolls, pens and parchments; it would be of no value. He would be worthless. Also, how would he live? How would he survive? How would he earn a living without his sight? He would not be able to sew the goatskins together. He would not be able to mend and repair tents. The thought of a life of blindness made him question whether he wanted to live?

The Rabbi prayed and prayed. He prayed without ceasing. It was as if he needed to be cleansed from something within him but what that something was, he did not know.

The Rabbi was proud of his achievements. He was a Pharisee. In fact, he was more than just a Pharisee. He had a heritage that meant he was revered and honoured by his peers. His parents were righteous people who had kept and honoured the Law of Moses. Even though they lived in Tarsus far away from Jerusalem they had raised him as a Torah scholar just as if they had been living in Jerusalem. At his Bar Mitzvah they had arranged for him to move and live in Jerusalem to be in the Rabbinical School led by Gamaliel. Whilst there, the Rabbi was the envy of many because of his sharp attentive mind and his ability to grasp concepts and ideas very quickly. He was able to comprehend the most complex rabbinical arguments about the law and its interpretations.

He was also from the tribe of Benjamin. It may not have been the largest and most important tribe next to some of the others, but their founder and patriarch could boast that he was the only patriarch born in the Promised Land. The Rabbi did not often reveal his inner thoughts, but he secretly wished that he had been born in Bethlehem, not near it as Benjamin had been, but actually in it. Bethlehem, the town that the Messiah was to come from.

The Rabbi was also a citizen of Rome, but he placed no value upon that citizenship. Rome had trampled on all that was precious to him. However, it was useful at times though, being a Roman citizen. He used it to his advantage to gain what he needed or wanted, but other than that, he kept very quiet about his citizenship to the empire that was Israel's enemy.

The Rabbi's finest accomplishment to date after being recommended and welcomed by his teacher Gamaliel into the prestigious circle of the Pharisees was to be chosen for this mission. But now he was blind. Useless.

He sat in silence letting the tears flow freely. He recalled his Bar-Mitzva. His parents had been so proud of him as he stood on the bimah to read from the sacred scroll. He had stumbled over the first few words with so many people, his parents, his sister, his friends, all staring. Then he paused and in those few seconds was flooded with peace and confidence. He then continued without any further hesitations. Many stared as he read so confidently, so fluently. His father and mother were so proud of him. Even his sister was, though she would never admit it. That was her way. But would he ever see to read again?

The Rabbi pulled his prayer shawl around him and began to focus on his prayers, but his mind kept wandering.

The Lord had revealed himself as Jesus. The Rabbi was trying to grasp how Jesus could be the Lord. How could he be God, or be the equal of God, or the son of God?

The Rabbi returned to the Psalms and his prayers. They brought him comfort and strength.

To the Rabbi the Torah, the Prophets, the Writings were the reasons for living. The Torah to him was not just instruction in living but a means of expressing and demonstrating his love for God. This was why it was so important to be a Torah student. It was his life, his passion, his purpose for living and breathing. He had inherited this love for God from his mother and his passion for the Law from his father. He loved the Lord his God with all his heart, soul, mind and strength. His life's purpose and calling, was to study, to love, to honour, and to respect God.

Under his prayer shawl he prayed to the God he had willingly devoted and dedicated his life to, but his mind wandered.

Jesus had appeared to him.

In the dark the Rabbi lay on his bed. He recited the Psalms quietly to himself. As he began his next Psalm he stopped. He then repeated the words:

> *The Lord said to my lord,*
> *"Sit at My right hand,*
> *until I make your enemies*
> *your footstool."* Psalm 110:1

'Who is King David's Lord?'

'Is the Messiah David's Lord?'

'Is David's Lord the Messiah?'

'Jesus...?'

His thoughts wandered back to the road when the Glory had suddenly flashed around him. This was the first time he had ever experienced the Glory. What had shaken him to his very core was not the Glory, nor the voice from heaven, but whose voice it was. 'I am Jesus!', the voice had said. That was the last thing the Rabbi had expected to hear.

He would have been awestruck if it had been God who had spoken, but it was Jesus. The Rabbi was...speechless...confused...Jesus, Jesus who was dead, had spoken from within the Glory.

The Rabbi whispered to himself, 'How could he be...Is what the heretics say actually true? Is he alive? Has he been raised from the dead? Is he the Promised one, the Messiah?'

He paused, was deep in thought for a few moments and then said, 'And not just the Messiah but the son of God?'

The Rabbi went quiet again pulling his prayer shawl over his head. 'Impossible!' he quietly muttered.

The Rabbi woke, stiff and cold. He did not know how long he had been kneeling by the side of the bed. He could not even remember leaving the bed to kneel. He listened and heard no-one moving so he assumed it was still night or very early. In his blindness he couldn't even distinguish any change between light and dark. It was as if his eyes had been removed. There was no pain, nothing. He remembered the words of the Psalmist:

> *A shepherd called "Death" herds them,*
> *leading them like mindless sheep straight to hell.*
> *Yet at daybreak you will find the righteous*
> *ruling in their place.*

Every trace of them will be gone forever,
with all their "glory" lost in the darkness of their
doom.
Psalm 49:14

Though they have the greatest rewards of this
world
and all applaud them for their accomplishments,
they will follow those who have gone before
them
and go straight into the realm of darkness,
where they never ever see the light again.
Psalm 49:18-19

The Rabbi said to no-one in particular, 'Is this what hell is like? Being led around by a servant. Lost in the darkness. Total darkness. With normal life suddenly ripped away from you. All my accomplishments mean nothing now. Will I ever see light again?'

He stumbled to his feet and felt his way to a chair. He slumped into it. He sat there not knowing what to think. His life was changing. The Rabbi didn't know whether it was for the better or not. And what was the change? He wasn't sure about that either. He had many questions but still no answers. He felt for a few moments as if he was living in hell on this earth before death.

In the silence he remembered how he had always enjoyed going to the Temple in Jerusalem at the Festivals. Such joyous times. He remembered how all the pilgrims had rubbed shoulders and knocked each other around, but never with any malice, only with excitement and joy, as they entered through the gates into the city. How could they all fit in to that small city? And the children. You were always falling over them. He had never missed a service at the Temple during the Festivals. When the Levitical singers in the Temple sang praises to God it was like listening to an angelic choir. The Rabbi had spent all of his spare time visiting the holy sites in and around Jerusalem. The tomb of David. The valley where the prophets were buried. So many reminders of the golden age of King David. During the Festivals there were so many people in the Temple all hoping for a new future. All looking for the Messiah who would come and establish the Kingdom, the Kingdom of God, the Kingdom of Israel.

He remembered his last Passover in Jerusalem. Everywhere there was hope, hope of a redeemer, of a Messiah. Things would be different then when he finally arrived. No more Romans. No more apostasy. No more doubts. Visiting the city and the Temple had filled him with such a zeal, a hope, a passion for God, for his promises, for his prophecies.

As the Rabbi was sitting deep in his thoughts, he did not know that the sun was rising, a new day was dawning. He was unaware of the change until he began to feel the warmth of the sun in the room.

Chapter Nine

A new day dawns.

The Rabbi called for the servant to attend to him as he wanted and needed to begin a new day.

The servant assisted him, helped him, and cared for him as if he was a patient being nursed after an illness. Since the Rabbi had arrived at the house the servant had ministered to him as a father would do to his child who was still too young to care for himself. The servant throughout his duties remained quiet as he did not want to draw any unnecessary attention to himself. The servant often thought about why the Rabbi was in Damascus; to arrest the followers of Jesus. Would the Rabbi arrest him if he knew? Would Judas protect him or turn his back on him?

The servant finished and guided the Rabbi back to the seat near the window. The breeze at this time of the day was cool but not as cold as when it came down from off the mountains. The Rabbi sat quietly. He felt, well what did he feel? So many emotions. He had a peace within himself that he could not understand nor explain. But there was also a turmoil. It was as if there was a raging storm in his soul. How could peace and turmoil exist side by side within him? He pondered but was unable to reach any conclusions.

A few weeks ago, he had left Jerusalem to travel here. One of those travelling with him had laughed at him because he had been so consumed by hatred, murder even, against anyone who mentioned the name of Jesus. They had not seen him so angry before about anything. And now that anger was gone. It was as if someone had snatched it out of him.

The Rabbi began to feel shame. He had been so proud of his devotion and love to God. He felt shame because he had taken the lives of people, not the heathen, not the gentiles, but the lives of his own people, God's people, God's chosen ones. He felt ashamed of what he had done to his own people. He loved Israel with a passion but the way he had acted had showed anything but love for the nation he was so proud of.

When Judas had completed his morning prayers, he normally went to enjoy his breakfast but this morning he headed straight for the room of his friend. Judas spoke with the servant for several minutes about the Rabbi. How was he? Judas wanted to know everything, every small detail. Judas entered and found his friend seated near the window. He was looking out as if he was enjoying the view. Judas wondered if the Rabbi had regained his sight in the night. The physicians did not know whether this blindness was temporary or what. Sometimes they were useless despite their learning. They had even dared to hint that if the Rabbi repented...and then they went silent keeping their thoughts to themselves as if they realised in whose home they were, and also who their patient was. Judas greeted his friend who turned towards the voice.

The Rabbi was not ready to talk and share. He, however shared a little with Judas so as not to offend him. They had become close over the years. Judas could sense something about the Rabbi. He was different. But how? Broken? He did not ask anything further of his friend. The servant noticed how Judas embraced the Rabbi. He had not seen his master so demonstrative before. Judas left without looking at the servant. He was focused on his friend. He left the Rabbi to his prayers.

Judas pondered as to why God had revealed himself to his friend. Why? What for? And why had he blinded him? Was he being punished as Miriam had been when she offended God by speaking against Moses? Had the Rabbi sinned and now he was being punished? But what could he have done for he was the epitome of righteousness? 'If the Rabbi has been judged and blinded for his sin, what will happen to the rest of us?' muttered Judas.

The house was getting full, and it was not yet midmorning. Visitors were coming to meet with the Rabbi, but none were shown into his room. Judas met them all and talked with them. Some went away whilst others stayed. Judas was known for his hospitality and his table was always full. His was a table that was not known for its extravagant fare but for the discussions, the debates about the law, the interpretations of the prophecies and the most discussed topic of the day, the promised Messiah, and the Kingdom he would usher in with his arrival.

The servant had always enjoyed the scholars and Torah students visiting his master Judas. He looked forward to them because there were always lively debates and many passionate or rather heated discussions that often went late into the night about the prophecies about their land and their future as a nation.

The servant normally looked forward to the Rabbi's visit as he would challenge and debate and would often speak with some of the older Pharisees and more experienced Rabbi's as their equal. He could hold his own with a passion even when he was wrong which was not often. But this visit had turned out to be different. The Rabbi had been brought into the house blinded by something on the journey. He was normally outgoing, talking to everyone but now he never spoke. The Rabbi had changed. Something had changed him, but what?

And now the Rabbi wanted to be alone. Why was he seeking solitude from all his visitors some of whom he knew so well? What had really happened to him on the road into the city? The servant had heard the rumours about how the religious leaders were persecuting the followers of Jesus, but he never had thought that someone like this Rabbi would be the persecutor. Had be become involved with the wrong crowd in Jerusalem? He once was so caring and carefree, a man who loved life. He would never have hurt anyone.

The servant waited at the door in case he was needed. He had been asked by Judas to always be near to the Rabbi in case he needed anything. The servant enjoyed working for Judas. Judas was a man who respected his servants and asked them to do things, he never demanded or shouted. This was why he also liked Nicodemus when he visited. Judas was like Nicodemus. Nicodemus, despite being one of the greatest teachers in Israel, was always very quietly spoken as well as kind. He always spoke to all the servants. He even spoke gently to those who were clumsy and new.

The servant heard the Rabbi raise his voice. He began to move to attend to the Rabbi, to help him, but then he recognised the words the Rabbi was speaking. They were from the prophets.

The Rabbi stood and began to pray to the Lord, and he fell silent. 'Who is my Lord?' he quietly asked himself.

He knew it was Adonai, the Lord, the God Almighty. But Jesus had said he was the Lord. The Rabbi had no doubts that he had been spoken to, he had clearly heard a voice, but the voice of Jesus?

Could what he had been fighting against actually be the truth? Could this man actually be the Messiah? Could he be the Lord? Was he...is he...divine?

The Rabbi remained very silent, but his mind was racing and his thoughts within him felt very loud, so loud that he felt the servant must be hearing them.

How many Pharisees believed Jesus was the Messiah? None! How many accepted his divinity? None! The Sanhedrin had examined this man Jesus. They pronounced him guilty and declared to all that he was not the Messiah. Isaiah had said that the servant was to suffer. The nation of Israel was to suffer, not the Messiah. They had suffered when their first temple was ransacked. They were a people destined to suffer. That's why they were waiting for the Messiah. To stop the suffering. To restore the nation back to its rightful place as the head and not the tail, to be above Rome and not beneath their iron clad feet.

The Messiah was to rule and to reign. Not die. The Messiah was to conquer and establish God's Kingdom on earth. Not be crucified.

The Rabbi put his head into his hands and sighed. Could the teachers be wrong? Could the Sanhedrin have got it wrong? Could the servant that suffered in Isaiah not be the nation but the Promised one, the Messiah? Could those passages actually refer to Jesus? Could Jesus who was crucified for blasphemy really be the Messiah we are all waiting for?

'But', said the Rabbi, 'How could the Lord be crucified?' As soon as these words had passed his lips the Rabbi blurted out, 'This is absurd! Ridiculous!'

'How could the Lord be crucified?' he continued, 'How could God's son die?'

'God is eternal'

'If God had a son, he too would be eternal not mortal!'

He sat down with such force it was as if he was in a court room and had finished presenting his case. His voice and posture said, 'there is no evidence that you can bring to make me change my mind.' The Rabbi added forcibly, 'God did not die! God, nor his son...or whatever...did NOT die!'

The servant had not heard what the Rabbi had been saying as he had been relieved of his duties for a short while as he had been asked by the housekeeper to go to the market to collect some of the produce needed for the evening meal. The servant was often sent to the market. He could be trusted to select the produce required rather than accept what the tradesmen wanted to get rid of. The merchants knew that many of the servants in the city were easy prey and so raised the prices and sold to them the damaged fruit or inferior produce. The servants did not care. Why should they? It wasn't their money.

The Rabbi's travelling companions knew what food he enjoyed, and they wanted to ensure his favourite meal was prepared for him that night. They all wanted to help him, perhaps his favourite food would encourage him to eat. He had not spoken nor eaten since he had arrived. He did not seem to be in any pain. He was not ill. One of his companions said that it was as if the incident on the road had ripped the heart out of him.

The servant had left the house and entered the hustle and bustle of the street. He did not have far to go to the market. He looked up and down the produce when suddenly a firm hand was upon his shoulder and a deep voice, full of authority, said, 'Found you at last you rascal!' The servant froze, his secret was out, now he would be thrown out of the synagogue and imprisoned. The Temple Police had found him!

The servant then realised to whom the voice belonged as it broke out into laughter. It was old Ananias. He was like a father or rather a grandfather to many of the men in the city who were followers of Jesus. The servant smiled. He loved Ananias. Since the servant had become a believer, he often went to his home to meet together with all the other believers, to break bread and to pray. Ananias knew that the Rabbi had arrived and wanted to know how the servant was faring as it was fast becoming common knowledge or gossip as to why the Rabbi was in the city. The servant shared what information he had and hurried back to deliver the produce to the housekeeper and return to his post. Serving the one who had come to persecute them.

The servant helped the Rabbi into the courtyard, and seated him in an area that was secluded, hidden away from any visitors who may have been wandering around. The Rabbi could feel the warmth of the sun on his face. The sun was high enough to reach over the tall walls of the house into parts of the courtyard. He was grateful for its warmth. It helped him not to feel so lonely.

The Rabbi knew he needed help.

But it was not people he needed. He had his travelling companions and Judas along with the many visitors seeking to talk to him, but their voices and their words pushed him further into his loneliness, into the darkness.

He wanted to run. He needed to escape. He wanted to turn back the clock to when he had lived with his parents safe in their care. He wanted to return to his days as a student when he sat at the feet of the great teachers, safe in their debates and questions. He wished he could go back to the time before he started this awful journey. He wanted to run and live in the past. He wanted to forget that moment when he had met the Lord.

But he couldn't escape. He couldn't forget.

And a part of him didn't want to. Although he was perplexed, there was something within him that was stirring. Something deep within him was coming alive and he wanted to understand and know what it was and so discover what was happening to him. The mystery of what it could be was beginning to consume his thoughts.

The Rabbi heard the voices of children. He felt so vulnerable. He didn't know they were by his side until he had heard their squeals of laughter. They were Judas' children. They meant him no harm. In fact, they did not notice he was there as they were lost in the game they were playing, but their sudden appearance made him feel so vulnerable. He realised that he did not know what was going on around him. He could not see. He called for the servant. Where was he? The Rabbi began to panic and feel afraid but then the voice of the servant calmed him. He had been nearby all the time, watching and waiting. The Rabbi asked to go back inside. He felt secure in his own room.

The Rabbi stared, transfixed. The servant looked from the doorway and wondered what he was looking at, or what he thought he was looking at. The Rabbi had not moved for a long time.

The Rabbi was deep in thought or in turmoil, he was not sure which it was. His very life was under review. He had been brought up to challenge, to question, to debate, to form, to reason, to believe. Line upon line. Precept upon precept. And now he was doing this to himself, to what he stood for, to his faith, to his beliefs, and to his God.

The words kept coming back to him

"I am Jesus, whom you are persecuting".

The Rabbi examined his motives. In his zeal to cleanse the House of God, the nation of Israel, he began to seek out the blasphemers, the unbelievers, those who were against the Law of Moses. The breakers of the Covenant.

The Rabbi quoted the Psalms:

My zeal has consumed me,
because my enemies have forgotten Your words.
Psalm 119:139

The Rabbi said, 'Lord, I was very zealous for your word, your law, your righteousness. I saw all who did not reverence your word, worship you, uphold your law, and build their lives on and around your

Covenant, as your enemies and therefore as my enemies.'

The Rabbi said:

Your word is pure and true;
therefore Your servant loves it.
Psalm 119:140

The Rabbi reflected on how, in his love for God, he had upheld the teachings and the traditions of the people of God, the children of Israel. He reflected on how in his desire for purity, holiness, perfection he had wanted everyone to be united in what they thought, said and believed about God. He had such a deep love and respect for God's word, his Torah, for the truth.

The Rabbi quoted the Proverbs:

The fear of the Lord is the beginning of wisdom,
and the knowledge of the Holy One is
understanding.
For by me your days will be multiplied,

and the years of your life will be increased.
If you are wise, you will be wise for yourself,
but if you scorn, you alone will bear it.
Proverbs 9:10-12

'Lord,' the Rabbi said, 'You know that I fear you. You have blessed me. You have made me wise. You know I have never scorned your word, your teachings, your wisdom, your correction.'

Jesus had also said,

'It is hard for you to kick against the goads.'

But the Rabbi couldn't help but think and speak out loud, 'Lord, it was you who was kicking against the goads. It was you who was against the traditions handed down to us from David, from Moses and from Abraham. It was you!'

The Rabbi began to scream as if he could not contain something that was seeking to escape. 'You', the Rabbi screamed amidst sobbing, 'It was you who upset the Temple, God's Holy sanctuary. You threw out all those who were helping the people worship by selling the animals the law demands! You were the one who allowed your disciples to profane the Sabbath. Why? Why?'

The startled servant jumped assuming that he had been called by the Rabbi. He had been dozing and was suddenly awakened by the Rabbi calling him, or so he thought. When the servant realised he was not being summoned he waited near the door. Waiting to be called, waiting to serve. And in his waiting, the thought about being arrested.

This time the Rabbi, amidst his tears, groaned. He groaned out of frustration; he groaned out of his inability to hear that something, that quiet voice deep within him. He groaned because the words he heard from those around him showed that they did not understand the true darkness he was in and battling against, the darkness he didn't want to live with. He groaned because of what he had just said.

The Rabbi's thoughts turned to the road again. Jesus had said that he was the Lord. How could he be God or the son of God? He was a man who had been crucified. The Rabbi remembered that one of the accusations against Jesus at his trial was his claim to be the son of God.

The Rabbi asked,
'Is Jesus God's son?'
'Are you God's son?'
'Well, are you?'

He had many questions. Had God hidden these facts from him, or had he been blinded to the truth? And what about the followers of Jesus? Why did they follow him? What had they seen in him that they were willing to risk everything for?

The Rabbi whispered in prayer,

'This has been my whole life. Studying your word, your ways. I have been very willing and very obedient to all of your word. The things your word says I have known and experienced. Your word has revived me. Your word has refreshed me. I know you have taught me because I have wisdom and knowledge beyond my years. Your word has strengthened me. I have been faithful to you and to your word. If you are the Lord, the Messiah, how did I miss it? Miss you? Why didn't the good news that these people talk about become good news to me? Why was I blind to the truth about you when I was seeking more of the truth?'

The evening meal was ready. The Rabbi's favourite food had been prepared. Judas went to visit his friend. The servant greeted his master as he approached and entered the Rabbi's room. Judas stood just inside the doorway and entreated his friend to come and eat. The Rabbi spoke and explained to his friend that he would not eat until a messenger from the Lord had come to bring him a message from the Lord. This was the first time that Judas had heard that the Rabbi was expecting someone. A prophet of God was coming to his home to visit his friend. Judas plied his friend with many questions, but the Rabbi was hesitant about saying anything further and gently explained to his friend that he needed to fast, to pray, to prepare himself for the one who would reveal to him what the appearance of God's Glory was all about. The Rabbi did not dare say anything further. What could he say that Judas would understand for the Rabbi himself didn't really understand what was happening? Judas blessed his friend and politely withdrew, nodding to the servant as he passed.

Judas went back to his table, to his guests. Blessed by the thought of a prophet visiting but who was this prophet? He did not know who that could be. To his knowledge God had not spoken through prophets for several hundreds of years. Were there any left in the Land? Judas was excited, God was on the move. Had the time come for the revealing of the Messiah? He knew his friend had had an encounter with God and that God was dealing with him, doing something. But what was that? It was a mystery.

Judas was also frustrated. He wanted to advise his friend. Support him, encourage him. But words failed him. He felt helpless. He too had many questions. But the question that perplexed him the most was the blindness. Why had God afflicted him in this way? How had he sinned to cause such a judgement to fall upon himself?

'But Jesus, but Lord, whoever you are', the Rabbi stumbled in frustration because he didn't know how he should address the one who had spoken to him on the road.

He paused not sure how to continue and then he formulated his question, and, in his darkness, he uttered it quietly to the darkness.

'How can you be the Messiah? You were not born in Bethlehem?'

'You are, or you were, from Galilee. From Capernaum.'

The Rabbi was frustrated. 'Even if you are who you said you are, the prophets declare otherwise.' The Rabbi did not know how loudly he had spoken these words. The servant heard him.

The servant turned to enter the room to speak with the Rabbi. He wanted to tell the Rabbi the truth about his Master. He knew that Jesus had been born in Bethlehem. He remembered his first visit to Jerusalem as a believer in Jesus. It was during Passover. Ananias had taken him to meet the apostles. Peter greeted them and had spoken about how the Holy Spirit had fallen upon them at Pentecost. James, one of Jesus' brothers, shared about Jesus and they also met Mary, the mother of Jesus. She always talked with any believer who asked her about her son. She loved to talk about the wedding in Cana, but the story the servant loved to hear time and time again from her was how the angel had appeared to her. The servant loved nothing more than listening to the stories that Mary, Peter and all the others were always ready and willing to share. The servant thought that if the Rabbi could hear these stories, then he too would know who Jesus really is.

The servant, who was always ready to speak up about his Master, felt the Holy Spirit within him restrain him. The servant felt that this was not yet the place nor the time to talk with the Rabbi about Jesus.

He knew it was not fear that held him back but respect for that inner voice of the Holy Spirit guiding him. He stepped back as if to allow the Rabbi some privacy.

The servant remembered the year that Judas had decided to stay in Jerusalem after Passover until Pentecost. Their stay in the city was extended that year. The servant and one or two others from the house were needed to stay with Judas and his family whilst the remainder of the house returned to Damascus. Judas had spent most days at the various Rabbinical Schools around the city he had contact with. This gave the servant many free hours during the day and so he spent much of this time with the church helping serve the daily distribution of food to the saints. It was here that the servant had met Philip, one of the deacons, who had taken him under his wing. Philip and the other deacons saw that God's hand was upon the servant in a special way. 'What could God be calling him to?' they often discussed amongst themselves. Philip had invited him to his home for the midday meal to meet the women he loved but teased, his wife and four daughters. The servant had grown fond of the elder daughter. He thought about her and wondered where they were now. He had learned from the saints who were sheltering with Ananias that Philip had left Jerusalem with his family, but where they were, no one knew nor even if they were still alive.

The servant had been so lost in his thoughts that he had not noticed that the Rabbi had arisen and was slowly trying to move across the room. He heard the Rabbi stumble against a table and quickly moved to guide and help him. As the Rabbi tried to grab something to support himself his prayer shawl slipped from his shoulders onto the floor. The servant helped the Rabbi. He then picked up the shawl and placed it in the hands of the Rabbi. No words were spoken. The servant straightened the table and noticed the Rabbi had not even drunk anything since he had arrived. He knew the Rabbi was fasting food for he had overheard him mention this to Judas. But water as well. The servant wondered how long this would go on for. How long could it go on for?

The Rabbi was comforted by the weight of the prayer shawl. It was familiar. It was security. Even so, the familiarity and security it brought did not remove the turmoil within his soul.

The Rabbi wrapped his prayer shawl around him and covered his head. He bowed his head and slowly raised his arms and hands. He wanted to pray. He wanted to talk. His prayers were of great help to him. They helped him control his mind and his thinking. They helped bring peace into his soul. And also, they helped him process all the questions that he had. The list kept growing. The followers of Jesus proclaimed him as the Messiah, the son of God. He knew that in his heart this was what he was coming to believe but he needed to think these things through as they were not just challenging but changing his theology. This was something he was hesitant to do at first as all his beliefs about God, all the studying he had done were all Torah based, on the truth about the truth. So how could this be challenged and changed? But now he was beginning to see these things in a different light, the light of revelation. He knew this thinking would be considered radical by some, and blasphemous by others. However, to the Rabbi, it was the natural next step to take which excited but also troubled him.

He knew that he was changing. He was becoming one of 'them' rather than standing firm as one of 'us'. His emotions were also up and down. He needed peace. One moment he was filled with joy and excitement as to what was being revealed to him. The next moment, or even in the same moment, he felt as if he was all at sea, total confused, feeling very vulnerable, seeking something stable to hold on to physically, emotionally, and spiritually as he was drifting, not knowing where. It was as if he needed an anchor. The Rabbi wanted quiet, he needed peace because if he was to follow Jesus as his Lord, he needed to understand and have answers to his many questions.

'I am sorry Lord', he whispered apologetically, 'I need proof from your word.'

'I need answers.'

'I need to know in whom I have believed in.'

'I did – when I believed in the Lord, the Almighty – but a son – his son?

The Rabbi was very still and quiet for a long time. He then prayed:

> *To You, O Lord, will I cry;*
> *my Rock, do not be silent to me;*
> *lest if You were silent to me,*
> *then I would become like those who go down to the pit.*
> *Hear the voice of my supplications*
> *when I cry to You,*
> *when I lift up my hands*
> *toward Your most holy place.*
> Psalm 28:1-2

Chapter Ten

The second night of darkness. The Rabbi realises another day has gone by as the servant lit the lamps. Why? he thought. What difference does it make? The Rabbi realised that the light may not have been for him but for the servant, for others in the house.

The Rabbi was quiet again. He was under his prayer shawl. He was listening to the noises as the house grew quieter and quieter. He was aware of someone at the door and assumed it was the servant. He imagined Judas at his final prayers of the day or was he still at the table in discussion with those visiting his house? He tried to sleep.

The Rabbi in his darkness was pondering his faith, his salvation. He bore in his body the mark of circumcision. A personal mark. A private mark. The mark of the Covenant he had with God, his Saviour and his Redeemer. He had faith in the merits of Abraham. The merits Abraham had gained with God through his faithfulness to sacrifice his son. Merits that passed to the faithful ones, the believing ones. The Rabbi had always known he was one of those faithful believers. The Rabbi's thoughts turned to Passover. The three pieces of bread represented Abraham, Isaac and Jacob. He worshipped the God of Abraham, Isaac and Jacob. The middle matzo, or middle piece of bread, on the table represented Isaac and was broken thereby rereminding them that Isaac had been broken on the altar that Abraham had made. There were various opinions. Did Isaac die or did the angel save him? The Rabbi knew it was conjecture and the sages had varied thoughts, but he erred towards the thought that Isaac had died by his father's hand and that God had raised him back up to life. 'Why not? Nothing is impossible for our God', he thought. 'And', he continued, 'Abraham knew by logic and reason that Isaac would be raised from the dead because of the promise God had made to him. The Rabbi paused, wondering. 'Using the same argument could Jesus have been raised from the dead?'.

The Rabbi's thoughts drifted back to his parents. He remembered the Passover meals from when he had lived with his parents as a young boy. The Rabbi smiled. It had been his duty during the meal to run to the door, when his father had nodded to him, to welcome in Elijah. He had always expected to see someone there. He smiled to himself as he remembered his disappointment when Elijah was not standing there waiting to be welcomed in. *No Elijah this year. Perhaps next year* he often said to himself. His mind drifted or was he being led?

Had he missed something? Was there something more? What was it? What could it be? Was there more? But what more could there be than the Law? Was there more truth yet to be revealed? But why had it remained hidden and why for so long? He had been circumcised on the eighth day. He was born as one of God's flock, God was their Shepherd. They had the law, the prophets, what more could there be? The Rabbi decided to ask the question.

'God', the Rabbi said, 'We are the apple of Your eye, Your chosen people. You have blessed us and revealed to us so much and given to us the Law, the Torah, the prophets, the Covenant. So, how could there be more?'

The Rabbi went very quiet. He knew what he wanted to say, to ask. Something he had never thought of before because to many it was considered blasphemy and to the Rabbi a few days ago he too would have considered it blasphemy. But now, that something deep, deep within him was forcing the thought into his mouth. He then, gasping for breath, muttered very quickly, 'God, is there more? Have we missed something? Is Jesus your son? Is he the Messiah?'

He then said it; 'And if there is more, what is that more? Have you lied to us all these years? Why didn't the prophets tell us there was more?'

The Rabbi regretted the way he had let his thoughts wander because he knew he was being disrespectful to God in questioning him this way. His God was Judge overall. His God was the King of the Universe, King of all Kings. But, deep, deep down inside of him there was a voice, and he knew it was not the darkness speaking. A small, very gentle whisper trying to say something he could hear but not quite hear, something he could discern but not quite discern. But he knew that was the answer to what he was seeking and asking. He muttered to himself:

As the deer pants after the water brooks,
so my soul pants after You, O God.
Psalm 42:1

The Rabbi raised his voice and the servant heard him say some words from the prophet Zechariah:

And I will pour out on the house of David and over those dwelling in Jerusalem a spirit of

favour and supplication so that they look to Me,
whom they have pierced through. And they will
mourn over him as one mourns for an only child
and weep bitterly over him as a firstborn.
Zechariah 12:10

The Rabbi rose from his bed and knelt on the ground
and asked, 'Is this what I am feeling? Is this what the
pain inside of me is? Is this why I feel as if I am crying
on the inside?'

The Rabbi bowed low to the ground and was
silent. Confused. Bewildered. 'Am I really mourning
for Jesus?'

The Rabbi was slowly beginning to understand
in a new, deeper way, what it meant to be the apple
of God's eye. The Rabbi was realising that how he
treated fellow Jews, whether believers in Jesus or not,
was a reflection upon the Lord himself. That was how
God judged his people. Not by their worship of him
but how they treated one another. And in this
revelation, he was also realising that his God had a

son, and that son was Jesus whom he had been persecuting.

The Rabbi fell silent again and was deep in thought, analysing his thoughts. Since he had met Jesus on the road, the Rabbi had begun to think about the Gentiles, the heathen, the nations of the world. He couldn't understand why he was thinking about them because they were mainly wicked people, without any hope, to be pitied, pagans. In the past he had spoken with other Pharisees about the heathen that were living amongst them in their land. Why did they choose to live with them? Some were slaves but what about those who were free? They were foreigners and always would be. They were strangers in their land, outside their covenant, and aliens to their God. They were tolerated in the synagogues when they expressed faith in God but as a people, they had no hope. But were they to have hope? The Rabbi realised that he was beginning to think about the nations of the world in ways he would never have dreamed of before. Had he lost his wits and his common-sense along with his sight? Could Rome be saved!

Sleep evaded the Rabbi. He frequently dozed but then woke up as if he had been shaken awake by someone or something that would not let him sleep. He wanted to sleep. To escape the weariness. Escape from his thoughts. Escape from the waiting. Escape from the heaviness that was weighing him down. The voice had said,

"Saul, Saul, why do you persecute Me?"

The Rabbi pondered again these words. In fact, he wondered, had he ever really stopped thinking about them? They kept ringing in his ears. How could he, in his zeal to protect the faith, have persecuted the one he was believing and waiting for? He knew what he had to do but still could not fully understand.

He repented.

He repented to the Lord.

He felt the tears quietly rise up within him, he did not fight to hold them back. It was as if they were washing him clean.

He repented of what he had done to those who believed in Jesus as the Messiah.

He repented of how he had treated the followers, the disciples, the believers.

Jesus had said that the Rabbi was persecuting him. He repented again.

The tears flowed freely.

The Rabbi began to realise how much he had hurt Jesus as he had persecuted, imprisoned, and executed his followers. The Rabbi now realised that to persecute the people was to persecute the one they believed in. The Rabbi thought about what he had done to this Rabbi from Galilee...who was Lord...who was becoming his Lord?!

The Rabbi knelt on the cold floor and repented. Jesus had said:

"Saul, Saul, why do you persecute Me?"

The Rabbi realised that even though he was persecuting believers, he had in fact been persecuting Jesus. When he had been imprisoning believers, he had been imprisoning Jesus. As he had been agreeing to their execution, he had been executing...the Rabbi stopped abruptly. He was beginning to understand.

The Rabbi wept and wept.

He could not stop shaking as the tears flowed. He was glad it was night, and the servant wasn't awake by the door as he faithfully was during the day, hour by hour, waiting to help and to serve him. The servant was gently snoring at his post. He didn't want the servant or anyone to see or hear him like this. He was so ashamed of what he had done. So ashamed of who he was. A few days ago, he felt that he was one of the most righteous of people alive but now he felt as if he was the greatest of sinners. He had fallen so far from God. Was there any hope for him? Could he be restored?

He repented and repented. He knew he could do nothing to earn the mercy and forgiveness he now so desperately wanted and needed. As he knelt, he wanted to do something to make amends, to do something for the one he had persecuted, and through the tears he muttered, 'Anything, I will do anything for you.' 'Anything, Lord.'

The Rabbi exhausted drifted into sleep.

The Rabbi awoke suddenly from his restless sleep. He opened his eyes and remembered his blindness. His heart was heavy, not just because of his blindness but because of his disturbed thoughts. The stoning haunted him. The Rabbi's sleep was disturbed by the images of the blood and especially the silence. The man had never cried out. He had never begged for mercy. He had never cursed God. He was silent as if he knew that this was his destiny and he welcomed it. There was no fear.

The other thing that was fixed forever in his memory was what the man had done. Bruised and broken, his bones must have been broken, he knelt in prayer. He moved and knelt. The Rabbi was not close enough to hear any words, but he had seen the look on the man's face. As he knelt, he winced as if his knees were causing him great pain. But then he saw a quick change come over the man's face. So peaceful, almost glowing. Could his expression have been one of joy? But joy was not an emotion that the Rabbi would have attributed to anyone who was being stoned.

The Rabbi began to think about the man they had stoned. Did he have a wife that grieved for him? Did he have children? How were they coping without a father? The Rabbi wished for a few moments he could turn back the clock. Once he would have wanted to do that to remove from his memory the sounds and the sights of a stoning. But now he wanted to turn back the clock because he saw the dying man as a brother, a fellow believer. In his darkness a light was shining on all the faces of the people he could recall whom he had arrested and sent to be executed. They were once just objects of his wrath. He now saw them in a different light. He belonged to them and they to him. He was one with them. Were they now looking down upon him? Had they witnessed what had happened to him on the road? Was he now here because of their prayers? He wanted to ask forgiveness from each one and be reconciled to them.

The Rabbi slowly massaged his head. It was aching and he felt exhausted. He lay back wanting to rest but also to think.

He snorted and woke up. He didn't realise that he had fallen into sleep. Was it for minutes or hours? He had no way of knowing. As he lay there, he realised his headache had gone and he felt relaxed. He began to think. Why would Jesus allow himself to be arrested and killed on a cross of all things? He had not been stoned as his follower Stephen had. Why had Jesus died this way? It was a cursed death.

The Rabbi drifted into sleep, awoke and continued with his thinking about the death of Jesus.

This thinking, dozing, waking, pattern continued for a long time.

He knew that Jesus was alive. He had seen him. The followers of Jesus believed he had been raised from the dead. The Rabbi believed in resurrection. He believed in the resurrection of the body. 'We will need a new body to house us in as we live in Paradise with our God in Eden' he had often said. He remembered his studies into the historical books about how the soldiers had buried one of their own in the tomb of Elisha. As soon as the lifeless body hit the enshrouded body of the old prophet, the dead soldier came back to life. It was usually a lively point for debate at the tables, who was more shocked and amazed, the dead soldier or his companions? No, resurrection was not a new concept or doctrine to the Rabbi. He kept going over in his mind all that he had heard, read and discovered about the followers of Jesus.

They preached about the need to repent and be baptised. This again was not revolutionary. The Rabbi had preached himself of the need for Israel to repent and turn back to God. Israel needed purity once again in the nation, in its worship. And, the Rabbi was known to have said on many occasions and had often been criticised for expressing that purity was needed in the Temple. Priests that were totally devoted to the Lord. The Rabbi was only a Pharisee, but he knew beyond any doubt that he was more fitted to serve at the altar then some of the priests. He would have been highly honoured to fulfil such a role, but he was not born into the right tribe.

Again, baptism was not a new concept to him. Baptism was cleansing. A removal or washing away of the old. Arising to the new. He knew all about this from his mother and sister because of their monthly visits to the baptismal pool. The Messiah when he arrived would also baptise. He would cleanse the nation, the people.

The followers of Jesus also spoke about how important the name of Jesus was, how it was the only thing that brought salvation. This was blasphemous. This was what caused his followers to face imprisonment and death. The Rabbi tried to understand why and how they came to this belief. This perplexed him. It did not make logical sense. His Torah trained mind kept hitting insurmountable obstacles and questions.

The Rabbi must have dozed again for he woke up. He lay there allowing his mind to access what lay buried deep within him. Then he remembered. The followers were known to meet together in secret. Why? He continued to delve into his memories and remembered. He really wanted to be back in Jerusalem in his rooms with his scrolls and notes to go over again all the evidence he had collected and what he had gained from his research into Jesus. But he was not at home, nor could he read. They had met together to take bread and a cup of wine to remember Jesus. Why use those symbols? Why remember Jesus who was alive with bread and a cup? Why remember his death when He was alive, and you could talk with him? It was as if they were remembering someone who was dead, or still dead, and someone not alive. The Rabbi thought about this and lay quietly praying, asking, wondering.

As he lay there it was as if, in the quietness, thoughts from within the depths of his memory were slowly gathering. It was as if they were snowflakes slowly falling to the ground and as they fell, he was seeing new patters, new thoughts. New revelations? Could this be the Jesus leading him? Could this be God showing him these new things?

He saw that there must be some connection between Jesus wanting his followers to remember him through some bread and a cup and Passover. At Passover they remembered the Pascal Lamb. What it did for them. What its blood meant to them. What its blood did for them. Could Jesus's death have a purpose? Could his shed blood have a deeper meaning then just his life blood being drained out of him? The Rabbi allowed his mind to explore these new patterns. These revolutionary thoughts.

Chapter Eleven

A new day begins to dawn.

Ananias waited for the next quiet knock at his door. He discreetly checked who it was and when he recognised the visitor, he let him or her in. Nothing was said. The door was quietly shut behind the visitor as another believer slipped into the courtyard. Ananias stayed at the door, listening, waiting. It was still dark. When all whom he was expecting had arrived he moved into the centre of the courtyard. The refugees in his house were also there, seated amongst the visitors. Even the children were there sitting snuggled up to their parents, struggling to stay awake at this early hour. His church had suddenly trebled in size. The servant was seated near the front.

Ananias explained that the rumour was true. The persecution had come to Damascus. Rabbi Saul was at the house of Judas. And then Ananias told the gathered saints what he had gleaned from the servant. How the Rabbi had been blinded on the road near the city. How he was in turmoil. How he was praying.

Ananias led the believers in prayer. He prayed for the Rabbi. He prayed for their own protection. He prayed that if they were discovered they would all have the courage to remain faithful and fearless to the end. Then he broke bread, gave thanks, and passed it around. He then took the cup and gave thanks and passed it around. They met like this most days. They met before the city woke. The believers could then come and go without being seen or missed. The believers were not afraid to be known for their faith in Jesus the Messiah. They were bold in their witnessing in the markets, but these meetings were in secret. It was when they could meet together to worship, to pray, to remember Jesus through the bread and with the cup, to meet with their Lord. Here they felt safe. Hidden away from the preying eyes of the religious leaders, away from the synagogues.

The servant was the first to leave. He bade the saints goodbye, Ananias blessed him, and then he hurried to get back. It would not be wise to be late this morning. Also, he needed to get back to watch, to observe, to be the eyes and ears for the church.

The Rabbi was roused by the warmth of the sun on his face. He opened his eyes to see and welcome in the new day and then he realised. He was blind. He had momentarily forgotten as he had awoken. He lay there feeling sorry for himself. He quietly wept, this time from self-pity. What was he to do? How was he to live? He lifted himself so he was leaning on his elbow, after a few minutes he sat up and felt for his prayer shawl. Instead of the prayer shawl he felt the blanket that had been draped over him. A blanket!

The Rabbi could not see the servant who kindly kept bringing things to him. No words were spoken but he could sense his presence and his care. The Rabbi pulled the blanket closer to him. The blanket that the servant had covered him with when he had dozed. He must have slipped into the room during the night.

The Rabbi wondered when something would happen. The voice had said to him,

"Rise up and go into the city, and you will be told what you must do."

He had heard the voice but had not seen the speaker.

He was trying to comprehend what had happened on the road.

The Glory had appeared, the voice had spoken, he stood up and was blind.

What was next?

Who would tell him what to do?

How could he do whatever it was Jesus wanted him to do if he was blind?

The Rabbi muttered, 'When Lord, when?'

The Rabbi remembered the words of Jesus,

'It is hard for you to kick against the goads.'

The Rabbi began to get angry. This was not who he was! He would never oppose the Lord. He had spent his whole life working for, and with, the Lord, never against him. The Rabbi looked back at his life. It was one of obedience to the Law. The Rabbi said to himself:

> *He said, "If you diligently listen to the voice of the Lord your God, and do what is right in His sight, and give ear to His commandments, and keep all His statutes, I will not afflict you with any of the diseases with which I have afflicted the Egyptians. For I am the Lord who heals you."*
> Exodus 15:26

He said 'Lord, I have always obeyed your word, your commandments. I have always done what is right in your sight.'

'If I have been kicking against the goads, then show me how? It is not possible.'

The Rabbi knelt in prayer. He covered his head, his eyes. 'Show me Lord, show me' he begged.

'Lord', the Rabbi cried, 'Why am I blind?'

The Rabbi remained silent and then he quietly recited the verse again.

The words from Isaiah the prophet then rose up within him:

> Keep on hearing, but do not understand;
> keep on seeing, but do not perceive.
> Isaiah 6:9

'Lord, have I been blind?'
'Lord, have I been deaf?'
'But how?'

The Rabbi had many questions. His mind began to fill with them once again. So many, too many. They were overwhelming him. He needed to write. But then he remembered he couldn't, and he screamed, 'Fetch me someone who can write'. The servant moved to get parchment and returned quickly to write what the Rabbi dictated. As the servant was writing he couldn't help but wonder how could the Rabbi think so fast? He would throw out scripture after scripture and note upon note whilst the servant was struggling to keep up. The servant felt the Rabbi was emptying his thoughts onto paper. The servant was used to writing letters or legal documents for the Rabbis but not this and at such speed.

When had the Rabbi changed his opinions on the scriptures, especially the prophecies about the Messiah? About Jesus? These were not the same things he used to teach on his previous visits. He was looking at the prophecies as if Jesus had fulfilled them. Was this Rabbi a secret believer too? Then why was he here persecuting believers? The servant just listened and wrote and wrote, growing more and more perplexed by what he was hearing.

The Rabbi asked the servant to pass him his bag. The Rabbi wanted to find his notes. The Sanhedrin had given to him information, reports, eyewitness accounts of the evidence that had been gathered against Jesus. He had been working on these reports and produced from them a list of the laws that Jesus had broken and a list of the things that he had done that were unacceptable within the fabric and culture of Israel. The servant found these notes for the Rabbi and then the Rabbi asked him to read them to him.

The servant began:

- Witnesses had come forward from his hometown in Nazareth declaring that he had blasphemed, and when they had attempted to throw him off a cliff to stone him according to the Law of Moses he had escaped

- Witnesses had come forward in Jerusalem to show that on at least on two occasions people had picked up stones to stone him to death for blasphemy in the Temple but he had escaped

- He casts out demons in the name of the ruler of the demons

- He added his own interpretation to the Law of Moses

- He allowed his disciples to pluck ears of corn on the Sabbath

- He and his disciples walked further than allowed on the Sabbath

- He healed on the Sabbath

- He could not give any signs to support his claims when asked

- He was not supported by any governing body or synagogue school within the nation when he was asked under whose authority he was ministering

- He did not teach his disciples the laws of washing

- He had no respect for the tradition of the elders

- He often and deliberately offended, rebuked and criticised the Pharisees in front of the common people

- He showed no respect for the teaching of the Pharisees, who were the carriers of Light and of God's Word to the people

- He openly challenged the Law of Moses on divorce

- He refused to allow those who were found guilty of adultery to be punished according to the Law of Moses

- He was critical and scathing of his elders and his betters

- He made himself unclean because of the types of people He chose to mix with

- He claimed to have the power to forgive sins

- A Pharisee named Simon invited him to his home, but he was rude to Simon and spent time with a woman, a known sinner

- He allowed sinners to be his disciples along with common people uneducated in the Torah schools

The servant paused to wipe the tears from his eyes. He quickly composed himself and continued:

- Another Pharisee who did not want to be named also invited him to his home only to be abused and criticised by Jesus in front of his guests

- One of the leading Pharisees, again he did not want to be named, invited him to his home on the Sabbath and he took advantage of the Pharisee and abused his hospitality by working on the Sabbath by healing another guest

- He snubbed the Pharisees when they asked him to correct his disciples as they organised a procession with palm branches on the Mount of Olives during Passover showing a lack of respect for God's Feasts

- He had an incorrect understanding of the Kingdom of God

- He disrupted the worship and prayers in the Temple by upturning the tables in the courts

- He had mixed with Samaritans, spent time in their villages, and even slept in their homes overnight

The Rabbi held up his hand, 'Enough' he said. The Servant stopped and laid the papers down. He too had had enough. 'Leave me' the Rabbi said, 'and put those papers back'.

The servant obeyed the Rabbi and as he left, he quietly shut the door, but he did not resume his normal post of watching and waiting to serve the Rabbi. He quickly walked to a secluded hidden part of the courtyard and wept. He couldn't contain himself. He couldn't hold back the tears. How could anyone write such awful things about the Messiah, his Saviour. What added to his pain and anguish was that these lists were from the legal documents from the Sanhedrin court. Why would they say such awful things? Who could actually have written them? It was quite a while before he was able to return to his post. He hoped that he had not been missed.

The Rabbi analysed his thoughts. Why was he thinking about gentiles? Israel was God's chosen nation. They were his chosen people. The Rabbi had always been taught by his parents that the Jews were the apple or the pupil of God's eye. He remembered how excited he was when he was able to read that verse in the language of heaven, Hebrew, not the Greek of the times but Hebrew, the language of eternity. God had chosen the Jews. He recited to himself:

> *Protect me like the pupil of the eye.*
> *Hide me in the shadow of Your wings,*
> Psalm 17:8

The Rabbi thought about his people, his nation, his land. He thought about how they were favoured because they were chosen. God had rebuilt their temple, their city and their nation after it had been destroyed by the Babylonians. They were back, restored, bigger and better, stronger and mightier than before. No other nation had ever been destroyed and recovered as they had.

The Rabbi recited with pride Isaiah 9:10,

The bricks are fallen down,
but we will build with hewn stones;
the sycamores are cut down,
but we will replace them with cedars.

Where were the Babylonians now? Gone for ever. History proved they were God's chosen ones, preferred above all others. And the Romans? They too would soon be gone when the Messiah arrived.

The words of the prophet Zechariah came to his mind:

And the Lord said to Satan, "The Lord rebuke you, Satan!" The Lord who has chosen Jerusalem rebukes you! Is this not a burning brand taken out of the fire?
Zechariah 3:2

When the Messiah comes, he will snatch us out of the hands of the Romans. Even though the Rabbi was a citizen of both nations, his loyalty was to Israel. Rome, and all the other nations, all were pagans. They were lost for they had no hope.

The Rabbi normally gave no thought to the other nations, but now he caught himself often thinking about them? Were they truly lost? Wasn't there any hope for them? This was so unlike him. Was he losing his mind? His mind was normally sound, solid, under control but since the road, that road, he felt as if he had lost control not just of his emotions but also his mind.

The Rabbi thought again about what Jesus had said to him on the road,

Rise up and go into the city, and you will be told what you must do.

He was now in the city. Who was to tell him what to do? When would they tell him? And what would they tell him?

The Rabbi was at a loss.

Jesus had given no hint as to what the answers to these questions would be.

He thought about how long he would have to wait. Who was he waiting for? Was it a prophet of God as Judas thought?

How long, and for whom? He already felt that he had been waiting too long. Someone known to him? A servant? A stranger?

His companions on the road with him had seen the light and heard a sound, some thought they heard a voice, and knew that something divine and supernatural was taking place but as to what, they had no idea.

He had not spoken to anyone about the experience. He avoided anyone talking to him about it. He needed time to reflect but upon what, he wasn't sure. He did know that he needed to think about Jesus as Lord, Jesus as the Messiah. This revelation to him had turned his world upside down.

What was Jesus going to ask him to do? Make restitution for all the wrong he had done against his followers? He was willing to do so but how could he do that? Some were in prison, some had died. Would Jesus want him to obtain the release of those in prison? Could he? Would the courts listen to him? He began to think of how he may be treated by the Sanhedrin. The hunter could soon become the hunted.

What could Jesus want from him and want him to do? Whatever Jesus commanded and asked of him, the Rabbi had decided that he would willingly do. Also, he wondered why would Jesus want him to do something for him, or serve him, or allow him to be one of his followers after the way he had acted towards him and his people? The Rabbi felt the chief of sinners. A few days before he had considered himself righteous and pure. Now he felt defiled and dirty. He had blood on his hands. He had called for the execution of his own countrymen. Some were from his own tribe. The Rabbi didn't know if he could live with himself. For the first time he was glad that he couldn't see for he didn't want to have to look at his own face in a mirror. He was ashamed. He felt worthless. He felt a failure for the first time in his life. He closed his eyes and wanted to escape from this nightmare. How much longer Lord, how much longer?

The Rabbi called for the servant. He asked him to look inside his bag for the letters that he had been given in Jerusalem. He felt ashamed of them as he held them. He felt them. They were no longer the blessing and the honour that he once thought they were. He felt unclean as he held them. He wanted to get rid of them. This was not who he now was. This was not who he wanted to be or known as. He held them up and said to the servant, 'Please burn them, here, now'. The servant obeyed and using the oil from the lamp destroyed the Rabbi's once precious documents.

The servant could hear the Rabbi praying using the Psalms:

My soul clings to the dust;
revive me according to Your word.
I have declared my ways, and You heard me;
teach me Your statutes.
Make me to understand the way of Your precepts;
then I shall contemplate on Your wondrous works.
My soul collapses on account of grief;
strengthen me according to Your word.
Remove from me the way of falsehood,
and graciously grant me Your law.
I have chosen the way of faithfulness;
Your judgments I have laid before me.
I have stayed with Your testimonies, O Lord;
may I not be put to shame.
I will run in the way of Your commandments,

when You set my heart free.

Psalm 119:25-32

The Rabbi had a long conversation with Jesus. To the Rabbi It was rather a one-sided conversation. He felt he was talking to and questioning someone who was listening but not responding.

The Rabbi quoted the prophet Isaiah:

He said, "Go, and tell this people:

'Keep on hearing, but do not understand;

keep on seeing, but do not perceive.'

Make the heart of this people dull

and their ears heavy,

and shut their eyes;

lest they see with their eyes,

and hear with their ears,

and understand with their heart,

and turn and be healed."

Isaiah 6:9-10

The Rabbi then prayed,

'Jesus, this does not make sense. We know God told Isaiah to tell the people that although they had heard the words of the prophets, they failed to understand and comprehend all that they had been told. The prophet was to tell the people that although they had seen amazing miracles and marvellous wonders that had occurred for their benefit, they failed to recognise that you had performed them. Lord, I know this, but this doesn't apply to me. How could it? My life has been one where I have chosen not to sin, I have not rebelled against you, I have done your will. So, why didn't I, a great scholar, one of the best students of the Torah, not see what those without education saw in you. They turned to you and were healed. What did they see I didn't or couldn't? I now look at your word and see things, things I never saw before. Why? What has changed? Why has it changed? Why wasn't I able to see these things before? Did you hide them from me? '

'But that can't be right because that means you blinded me to persecute you!'

'Why has it taken so long', he continued, 'for me to begin to see these things in your word? Why couldn't this have happened earlier to save all this bloodshed and heartache that I have caused your followers? Those I punished; they are also my people. I persecuted my own people because I thought I had the light, the righteousness, an understanding of your Kingdom and your ways, but they had the light. Why? Why are things like this? Why couldn't I see this before? Why couldn't we all have seen this earlier?'

The Rabbi moved carefully and slowly around the room shaking his head. 'Was this what you wanted? But why? Why did you allow this to happen to your chosen people? Is there any benefit in us having been chosen if this is how I am and what I have become? Why give me circumcision? That was to make me different, but I am no different. It didn't stop me rejecting you.'

The Rabbi stood still and raised his head as if he was looking into the throne room of heaven.

'According to the law I am legally righteous, I have proved I can keep your law perfectly, and what good was it? I rejected you, I even persecuted you. If you had been alive today, I would have dragged you off to prison and killed you. So, what good has any of my life been because this is where I have ended up, this is what I have become, a murderer!'

'Why choose me! I am no better than the gentiles. Rome killed you. I rejected you. We are all the same. What hope is there for me, for me, a fallen disgraced Pharisee?'

The Rabbi had been sitting very quiet for some time. The servant was not sure whether he was asleep. The Rabbi had his back towards the door. He was very still. He was very quiet as if he was asleep. In the silence the Rabbi spoke to the servant. His voice was quiet and gentle. 'Please, please come, sit down and write for me.'

The servant obediently entered and sat. He was ready to write. But the Rabbi said nothing.

The servant waited patiently. He knew better then to speak. He could see the Rabbi's face and it was as if he was thinking, formulating words, sentences. The servant was ready.

After several minutes the Rabbi spoke, or rather whispered,

'He appeared for a reason.'

'I appeared to you for this purpose.'

For several minutes the Rabbi continued to ramble. The servant wrote.

The servant thought that the Rabbi would have begun dictating a letter or his opinions on various sages or the scriptures. But this was... he didn't know what to call it or how to describe it. Unconnected words, a mixture of Aramaic, Hebrew, Greek and Latin. How many languages did the Rabbi speak? The servant was glad that he had been raised in Rome where it was not just the language of his home that he had learnt. He just faithfully wrote what he heard and hoped it would make sense to the Rabbi.

The Rabbi continued, 'A servant...I am a servant of the Lord...

...I am to be his servant...how?'

'To do what?'

'How can I serve you?'

'What can I do for you?'

'What could I do that he needs me for?'

'A witness...

a witness?...

of what you have seen...

I have seen him...

a witness to something, something else...

to what I will see of him...'

'What does this mean...

I will be rescued...

who from?

when?...

why?'

'Why do I feel I must go to the nations of the world?...

what am I to go for?

to do what exactly?'

The servant wrote. It was not difficult to keep up with the Rabbi as he was speaking a phrase or a word and then paused as if he was listening for the next word or trying to remember something. The servant did, however, have difficulty in trying to make sense of what he was hearing and writing. It was as if he was eavesdropping on only one side of a conversation, interspersed with reflections and remembrances of past conversations.

The Rabbi went quiet. The servant could see he was deep in thought. Was he thinking or listening?

The silence continued and then the Rabbi said quietly but very clearly,

'I am being sent to open their eyes. I am sent to turn them from their darkness to the light. I am to turn them from the power of the accuser to the Lord. They are to receive the forgiveness of their sins.'

And then the Rabbi went quiet again, but the expression changed to one of confusion, as if he was struggling to understand. And then he said,

'Can they be saved? Can they be sanctified? How? Can the nations, the heathen be as we are? You will sanctify them by faith? But what about good works? The good works of keeping the law, of caring for the poor, of giving to the orphans. Sanctify them by faith in you?'

The Rabbi went quiet.

The servant waited.

He quietly said, 'Thank You. Please put that in my bag.' And then he pulled his prayer shawl over his head and started to recite the Psalms.

The Rabbi needed quiet. He needed to be alone. He needed to reflect. He needed to...try and understand...the rhythm and poetry of Psalms would quieten his racing thoughts.

The Rabbi thought about what he had written on the parchment that was now concealed in his bag, or rather, what the servant had written for him. He still couldn't comprehend that he was blind. He reflected on his words and thoughts. 'It is as if I have changed my mind. But I haven't. It is as if my mind has been changed for me'

The Rabbi was confused. What was happening to him? He was thinking about things in such a way that he would have called heresy and blasphemy not long ago. What was happening to him? What was he becoming? His mind turned to Jesus.

'Jesus...how? Human and divine—impossible—but-nothing is impossible with our God. He said he was Lord. Is he? Was he? Could he be? Divine?'

The Rabbi hardly dared to think his next question let alone whisper it. 'Could Jesus be Divine?' But what does that mean? How was he? When did he become it? Had he always been it? Is he...no he can't be.

The Rabbi without realising it changed from thinking these thoughts to himself, to talking to Jesus, questioning him, challenging him.

The Rabbi's voice changed from a murmur to a whisper. His words that were whispered were now spoken clearly and loud enough for the servant to hear. The servant listened.

The Rabbi spoke louder, more forcefully, more confidently. He was quoting scripture after scripture. Prophet after prophet. The servant turned to see if someone else had entered the room, someone he hadn't noticed, but no-one was there. The servant looked at the Rabbi. It was as if he has having a scholarly debate with one of the sages. He had heard the Rabbi like this on many occasions over meals with the sages and the other Pharisees. But this time it was as if the Rabbi...well...had he lost his mind? Was he having delusions? Was he thinking he was back at the table debating the law and the prophets?

The Rabbi suddenly stopped. He said nothing further. The servant saw the Rabbi pull the prayer shawl over his head again. The servant heard nothing, but the Rabbi quietly whispered, 'I am sorry Lord. I am sorry for speaking to you like that. I repent. I need to know. I need to understand. There is so much I need to ask you. I have so many questions. Forgive me.'

The Rabbi asked the servant to take him into the garden within the courtyard where he could sit in the sun. The room was becoming oppressive. When he was seated the servant stepped back into the shade.

'Lord,' the Rabbi spoke quietly. The Rabbi was deep in thought but speaking quietly helped him. 'Lord, I can perceive you as Messiah, but divine? You were found guilty of that crime. Were you innocent? But you could only be innocent if you were divine.'

The Rabbi spoke, was he praying or just talking? It was difficult to say. The Rabbi, if he had been asked, would not have been sure either.

'Let us say you are divine. What does that mean? How were you or are you divine? When did you become divine? Or were you always divine? Were

150

you created? But if you are God or a part of God then you couldn't have been created. If you were not created but are God or a part of him, then you were...were you there at...so you must have...'

The Rabbi paused, and then the words spilled out. 'That would mean you were present in the beginning when the heavens and the earth were made. Were we made in your image, or did you present yourself to us in ours? You became flesh and blood...but how did the divine become flesh and blood?'

The Rabbi fell silent. He had a puzzled look on his face. 'And how can divinity cease to be and die. How did you die? I want to know why you died?'

'I want to know how you died. I know you were crucified but you were God so how could you die as we die? Did you go to Sheol?'

'But surely you by definition are greater than death?'

'Why did you have to die?'

'What was the purpose of your death?'

'Was it necessary?'

The Rabbi was lost in his thoughts again. Although he was quiet, with no words being spoken, his fingers were moving as if he was pointing to texts or comments on paper and then gesticulating as if he was having an argument or a debate in his mind.

And then he said, 'Did you ever sin? Were you sinless as the son of God? Were you as a man...or were you as God on the earth?'

The Rabbi argued with himself and sometimes with Jesus. He challenged and then counter-challenged. He was wrestling as he had been taught, as he had been brought up. He was not afraid to question, to challenge, to scrutinize everything. Hours had passed and the exhausted Rabbi began to doze.

As the Rabbi rested, he began to think about the Psalms. He had decided years ago to read a Psalm every day for the purpose of his personal edification. He had done this because he no longer wanted to deepen just his knowledge about God, but also the relationship, the intimacy he was beginning to experience with him. He had devoted many hours to doing this and had made copious notes on all the things that God had spoken to him about and all the things that inspired him. He had also journaled all his thoughts, which were really his heart-felt prayers. He knew God had been revealing more of the truth to him throughout this period. Sometimes he was not aware of anything but at other times he felt sure God was leading him and guiding him.

As he prayed, meditated, and wondered at what Jesus had said to him and what his followers claimed about him, the Rabbi began to think over some of the things he had written during the few years previous. Could it be that God had been trying to speak to him and see things afresh in the Psalms even then? He now began to think over his notes and tried to pick out any patterns or trends in his thinking and ideas. Perhaps they would show if and where God had been leading and guiding him. Could it be that God had been preparing him for this encounter with Jesus? Could it be that Jesus had been trying to reveal himself or preparing him for when he would reveal himself? The Rabbi felt as if he had been apprehended by God on the road to Damascus. The Rabbi pieced things together and could only wonder in amazement. For how long had God had had his hand upon him? And why? For what purpose or reason? The Rabbi felt it was not a coincidence that for the last few years of his studies he had been looking at the Psalms hoping to see the Messiah, and that he had also devoted himself to wanting to hear more of God's voice and deepen his fellowship with him.

He wished he was back at home with his sight so he could read over all his notes. He wanted to re-read all his writings to discern what God had been saying. Had God been speaking even then and he had misheard or not heard clearly enough.

The noise of children roused the Rabbi. He listened and heard them talking with the servant.

The Rabbi then thought about how outwardly nothing had changed but inwardly he had changed or was being changed. It was as if he was...being led...but he wasn't conscious of following anyone or anything. It was a mystery.

He realised that he was thinking about his life. His life now seemed but a dream. It felt no longer real. It didn't feel part of him anymore. It was as if on the road, when Jesus had confronted him, life had started all over again for him. It was a strange experience, but he felt more alive each day, as each moment passed even in his blindness.

He had so many questions, though for whom he didn't know. Yes, he did know, they were for Jesus. He wanted to meet Jesus again to sit, to discuss and to debate with him all the things that were whirling around in his mind. Things he needed to know and understand. He knew within his heart a faith in Jesus as the Risen Lord, as his Lord, was growing, and even as he thought this, he also could see himself standing outside of himself looking back at himself in disbelief. He was a Rabbi, a Pharisee. Him, Rabbi Saul, believing that Jesus was not just the Messiah but also the Lord. How absurd! But, in the same breath, how natural. He wanted to know Jesus. The Rabbi then spoke quietly into the breeze. 'Jesus, Lord, my Lord, I want to know you.'

'I will serve you, but I must meet with you again.'

'I have so many things to ask you.'

'Things I need to know about you if I am to serve you and die for you'.

The Rabbi was shocked and embarrassed. Why did he say that? What was happening to him? Where did that come from? Did he really say what he had just heard himself say? 'Die for you'. He knew he wasn't losing his mind but...the Rabbi quietly asked, 'Is it true Lord, is that what will happen to me? I will die for you as others have at my hands. Is that what will happen when Judas discovers what has happened to me? What I have become. Will he have me arrested and handed over to the Sanhedrin? The Rabbi despaired not of death but of how he would die. 'No, Lord, not crucifixion, please no,' he prayed with fear in his voice. As a Roman Citizen he would have to be handed over to Rome and then he would be at their mercy. He knew he would not receive any mercy from there and feared the worst. Crucifixion was rare but not unknown on Rome's citizens. May it be the sword Lord.

The Rabbi gripped the small table in front of him. He was shaking and wanted to steady himself. He had dreamt of growing old and being a respected teacher of Israel, one of the sages. He had hoped for a school of his own with his own group of students. But now he was to die, and perhaps within a few days, because he too was a follower of Jesus. Is this what the messenger who was to visit him would tell him? The when, and the where?

The servant led the Rabbi back to his room. He wondered if the Rabbi was ill and had a fever. He had watched him shaking at the table. He was shivering and even though he had sat the Rabbi in the shade it was not cold. He helped the Rabbi to find a chair and to sit down. The servant began to step back when he heard the Rabbi thank him and asked him to get parchment and pens to write for him. The servant sat at the table as those things were still there. He was ready for what he would be told to write.

The servant nearly dropped the pen. Did he really hear what he thought he had heard the Rabbi say? He looked at the Rabbi. The Rabbi looked in his direction and then quietly said, 'Why aren't you writing?' The servant stammered, 'I am sorry Rabbi, I was not ready and didn't hear what you said.' The Rabbi smiled to himself. So, it had already begun. The reactions. The shock on people's faces. The Rabbi couldn't see the servant's face but could imagine the expression and he could sense a change in the servant.

The Rabbi repeated, 'I want to consider how Jesus is the Messiah that our nation has been so long praying for, believing for, and hoping for' The servant wrote and reflected as he wrote how these were not jumbled incoherent thoughts as before. This was a well thought out rabbinical argument looking at prophecies, the psalms of King David, what the sages had said in the past. Line built upon line and precept upon precept. What the Rabbi was declaring now was a solid scholarly proclamation that Jesus was the Messiah and also the son of God. The servant smiled to himself, bemused.

When the Rabbi had finished the table was covered with several parchments and the servant's hand ached. The Rabbi asked the servant for the parchments and his bag. The Rabbi wanted to keep them close to him. He was not sure why. Was it for comfort? Was it to protect a secret? The Rabbi smiled. If that was the reason then if this servant was like any other, what he had heard would not remain a secret for long. But he didn't mind. He knew. He knew in whom he was now believing. He was ready.

The Rabbi quietly prayed:

> *In God whose word I praise,*
> *in the Lord whose word I praise,*
> *in God I trust, I will not fear;*
> *what can a man do to me?*
> *Your vows are on me, O God;*

I will complete them with thank offerings to You;

for You have delivered my soul from death,

even my feet from stumbling,

to walk before God

in the light of the living.

Psalm 56:10-13

Chapter Twelve

The day is nearly over, and the evening begins of the third night.

The servant heard these words before he was called away by Judas for his meal:

> *Teach me, O Lord, the way of Your statutes,*
> *and I shall keep it to the end.*
> *Give me understanding, and I shall keep Your law*
> *and observe it with my whole heart.*
> *Lead me in the path of Your commandments,*
> *for I delight in them.*
> *Incline my heart unto Your testimonies,*

and not for unjust gain.

Turn away my eyes from beholding worthlessness,

and revive me in Your way.

Establish Your word to Your servant,

so that You are feared.

Turn away my reproach that I dread,

for Your judgments are good.

Behold, I have a longing for Your precepts;

revive me in Your righteousness."

Psalm 119:33-38

The Rabbi quietly prayed,

'Thank you for teaching me your word.

I have been faithful to keep it all.

Thank you for giving me understanding.

I have observed all of your law with my whole being, my spirit, my soul and my body.

Continue to lead me, as my Shepherd, in your paths of righteousness.

They are my delight.

It is also my delight to be always in your will, in your way.

Thank you for inclining my heart to you and your word.

You have blessed me.

You have prospered me.

I have no cares for the things of this world but only for you and your word.

I have always sought to turn away from things that are worthless in your sight.

I desire to be holy as you are holy.

I want to be perfect as you are perfect.

Thank you for turning my eyes away from this world to your word.

My only focus is your word.

Revive me once again through your word.

You have made many promises to me.

I am your servant.

I want to serve only you and your will.

I seek only to establish your kingdom.

My desire that in me all your promises will be fulfilled and manifested so that your people, my people, will fear you, honour you, worship you.'

And then the Rabbi stopped. He was silent. He looked up. His eyes started to water. The tears started to flow down his cheeks.

The Rabbi turned away and said, 'Turn away my shame, turn away my shame Lord.'

'I am afraid, Lord...I am afraid of shame...of failing...of falling short...of not being accepted by you...I have worked so hard, I have striven, I have toiled...but I am so ashamed...of who I am...of what I have become...what am I to do?...what can I do?...Lord, I am wretched...Lord, I am miserable...Lord, I am a failure...I remember my past and I am so ashamed...what can I do?...I need to be delivered from myself?...is there any hope for me?...is there any future for me?...you want me to serve you but of what use to you am I now?...such a failure, such a worthless failure...what do you want me for?...I have nothing to give...I just feel so condemned...help me...'

The Rabbi woke and sat quickly upright. He was shaking. He didn't realise that he had been asleep, but the dream, it seemed so real. He looked up, even though he was blind. It was as if he was looking at someone. The Rabbi said, 'Lord, who is this man?' 'Does he live here?' 'Lord, what is happening?'

The Rabbi had seen a man in his dream, a man he did not know, a man he had never seen before, walk into the room where he was. The man had placed his hands over his eyes and spoken to him in the name of the Lord, the Lord Jesus. When the man removed his hands he could see, he could see! He could see again.

The Rabbi was excited, he felt hope, he felt strength returning, he felt the darkness lifting. The excitement began to rise within him. But this excitement was different to what he had experienced before. It was more of a joy. Something...not natural.

The Rabbi was turning over again in his mind the thoughts that kept rising up within him. 'What about the nations of the world?' 'What about the Gentiles?'

He remembered the words of Isaiah the prophet:

> *I the Lord have called You in righteousness,*
> *and will hold Your hand,*
> *and will keep You and appoint You*
> *for a covenant of the people,*
> *for a light of the nations*
> Isaiah 42:6

The Jewish people were a light in this dark world. They were a light to the Gentiles. Whenever Jewish families were not living within the Promised Land, they, wherever they lived, were considered as light bearers in the area of darkness of the area where they lived. The Rabbi knew this and believed it. All Jews are lights. The nation of Israel was the light of the world. Jews are lights in the world. But the Rabbi was beginning not to question the truth of that belief but how they had obeyed it. Israel and all Jews were to be separate so that their lights shone. The more separated they were from the darkness around them, the more they shone for God, for his Kingdom.

But the Rabbi was beginning to think that there must be more to this. The Rabbi thought about whether their isolated living was misguided. It was as if they were trying to protect a light that did not need protecting. They were protecting something that they were afraid of losing if they were not seen to be different. 'Are we not', thought the Rabbi, 'instead of just being the light that shines in isolation wherever we are, to take the light to the nations and help them to understand the light, even invite them into the light?' This was revolutionary to the Rabbi.

'Are we to share our hope with them? Are we to share our covenant with them?'

'But they are not chosen, we are your chosen people, so how can they be part of us?'

The Rabbi wrestled with these thoughts and concepts and what they could mean. He was thinking about what this would mean for him as a Rabbi if he shared these thoughts with some of his peers. 'Equality with the gentiles?' 'Never!' Even the Rabbi swallowed hard at the thought now he had actually uttered the words.

The servant heard the Rabbi say,

> *There is no other God but me, a righteous God and Saviour.*
> *By myself I have sworn, truth has gone from my mouth, a word that will not be revoked: Every knee will bow to me, every tongue will swear allegiance.*
> Isaiah 45:21,23

The servant wondered what the Rabbi was reciting. He did not know that it was from the prophet Isaiah.

The Rabbi prayed about how he was seeing these words in a new light. He asked Jesus if the words really applied to him. The Rabbi also asked Jesus if these words meant that one day, one day in the near future, every knee on earth would bow before him and acknowledge that he was the Messiah, the Saviour. The Rabbi thought about these words. Could this be true, and what would that mean?

The Rabbi awoke suddenly. He did not know how long he had been asleep, but he awoke because of his dreams or rather nightmares. They made no sense. He needed help. He needed to put his feet back on the Rock. He felt for his prayer shawl and couldn't find it. He called for the servant who was close by. He passed it to the Rabbi from where it had fallen. He then recited scripture verses from the Psalms:

I love You, O Lord, my strength. Psalm 18:1

'Lord, I love you' prayed the Rabbi.

'Lord, I love you. I thank you that you are my strength.'

The Lord is my pillar, and my fortress, and my deliverer;

my God, my rock, in whom I take refuge;
my shield, and the horn of my salvation, my high
tower.
I will call on the Lord, who is worthy to be
praised,
and I will be saved from my enemies.
Psalm 18:2-3

'Lord, you are my God, my Rock. I come to you now. I stand once again upon the Rock. I come to you for help, for strength. Help me to keep close to you. My thoughts disturb me. These thoughts are not from you. Help me. you are all I need. You are my shield, my protector, my salvation, my saviour, my high tower, my hiding place. Lord, I want to hide in you.'

The cords of death encircled me,
and the torrents of destruction terrified me.
The cords of Sheol surrounded me;
the snares of death confronted me.
Psalm 18:4-5

'Lord, as I was sleeping, I felt as if I was being dragged down. My thoughts were drowning me. It was as if darkness was filling me. I come to you, my Rock. I focus on you'.

The Rabbi continued to recite and pray. He then said, 'Thank you Lord, thank you for helping me.'

The Rabbi went silent.

'Jesus,' he said.

'Jesus, I want your mind. I want the mind you had when you were alive as a man, as flesh and blood. I want to think as you thought. I want to have the kind of thoughts you had. I want to be rid of the thoughts I have had. It is as if I am losing my mind, such confusion, such darkness. I want to have a sound mind, a mind that I can control. I want a mind that is always secure on the Rock, a divine mind. I do not want to think as I have thought in the past, as I thought again in my sleep, I want your mind. I want your thoughts. I want to know your ways. The prophet Isaiah said that your thoughts, your mind, is higher than ours. I want to be able to think as you think. That must be freedom. That must be true peace. I want you to renew my mind. Lord. How did you succeed where we fail?'

The Rabbi wondered when the man would arrive. He grew impatient. Patience was not one of the Rabbi's virtues. He wanted him to come quickly because he could sense the darkness was returning, that the joy he had felt was being overwhelmed and going. He began to have doubts, was it real? Was it my wishful thinking? Nothing has happened. Nothing has changed. No one has come.

He said, 'Lord, I believe it was real. I believe you have spoken to me through the dream. You have revealed to me that you want to use me. I am to be your servant. You will heal me. I refuse to let go of that promise. You speak through dreams and visions. I believe that. You have given me a vision. I believe that. I will not be moved by this darkness, this blindness. I hold on to the hope you have given me. I will be healed through this man, Lord. I have many questions, there is much I do not understand, but I know that your word will accomplish what you sent it to do. You are going to send this man to heal me. I receive it. I know your servant will come to me and all that I have been shown will happen.

The Rabbi was lost in thought again. Jesus was the Messiah he had been praying for, longing for, hoping for, looking for. But the Rabbi admitted to himself, 'This was not what I expected'. 'You were not what I expected.'

The Rabbi had been thinking about the scriptures. It was his way of life. Taught by his father and his mother, and the Rabbis. He had read and studied the prophets. 'So, why couldn't I see what you see?' 'How do we read the scriptures to ensure we are doing it from the correct perspective? To read what you, the Lord, inspired rather than what we have been taught to see as we read?'

He murmured to himself, 'How can we know what was in the mind of God as he wrote, as he dictated, as he inspired, so we read as God intended his words to be read, so we interpret his words as he intends us to understand and interpret them?' These and other similar questions were in the Rabbi's mind. He needed answers. He needed guidance. He needed help. 'If I have read them wrong, how do I read them right?' 'How do we know when our traditions are blinding us?'

The question that was now bothering the Rabbi as he sat there was not whether Jesus was who he said or claimed to be, but how can we know the mind of God, how can we rightly read, study, divide, and interpret the word of God? 'Can we do it?', asked the Rabbi. 'How do we do it?'

The Rabbi awoke. He sensed it was dark, it was night, why had he awoken? He felt restless and then reached out his hand for his prayer shawl. He sat up and pulled it not just around him but over him so that it covered him, consumed him. He whispered in prayer.

'Father,

I come to you for help, peace, restoration.

Cleanse me.

Restore to me the joy of your salvation.

I come to give you thanks.

You are my God.

You are my Lord.

You redeemed me.

You restored me to yourself.

I thank you that you are my God.

I am in fellowship with you.

You meet with me, and you speak to me.

Thank you.

There is so much to know.

How to be the person you want me to be.

Teach me.

Do not fill me with just knowledge of you but fill me with yourself.

I want to learn how to carry your presence.

How to be an ark, a temple, for your Spirit.

How to be consumed with you, focusing on you, your Spirit, your voice, your glory.

Consumed by you.

I want your fullness to dwell in me'

The Rabbi sat silent for a few minutes and lay back down.

He lay quietly, in his prayer shawl, in God's presence, in the peace, in the stillness.

He then said:

> *I seek Your favor with my whole heart;*
> *be merciful to me according to Your word.*
> *At midnight I will rise to give thanks to You,*
> *because of Your righteous judgments.*
> Psalm 119:58,62

The Rabbi was slowly realising that as he prayed, he was praying to Jesus as if he was the Lord. As if he had always been his Lord.

'Lord, there are some things I don't understand. There are some things I have been thinking about that don't make sense. What did you die for? Why did you have to die? You were welcomed into the city the Sabbath before your trial as the Messiah and King. You entered to establish the Kingdom of God. You came to establish your Messianic reign of a thousand years. So why die? What went wrong?'

The Rabbi then said to himself, 'But, if you are the Messiah you couldn't...it couldn't go wrong. So, what was really happening?'

The Rabbi continued,

'The Messiah was promised to be our King, our Saviour, our Redeemer. Our Messiah was to bring in the golden age of freedom allowing us to be the people we were called to be. So, why did you die? When you were executed, your dying was not a sign. You were the Messiah. Your dying was not a sign but a stumbling block. Entering Jerusalem as King and Messiah, now that was a sign', said the Rabbi, 'but not dying and especially not death by crucifixion. I see this as failure.'

At this point the Rabbi was screaming at Jesus out of frustration. 'When will you talk to me?'

The Rabbi was silent. Tears rolled down his cheeks. 'I am sorry Lord, I am sorry. Forgive me', was all he could say.

'Lord', the Rabbi said to Jesus. It was so spontaneous he had neglected to wrap his prayer shawl around him. He had been deep in thought and suddenly asked the question. 'Lord, why were you found guilty of blasphemy?'

The Rabbi recited verses from the Law that he knew so well:

> *Hear, O Israel: The Lord is our God. The Lord is one! And you shall love the Lord your God with all your heart and with all your soul and with all your might.*
>
> Deuteronomy 6:4-5

'Lord, how can you be the son of God? How can God have a son? Our God is one. How could Spirit give birth to flesh?'

The Rabbi tried to understand, tried to reconcile, tried to put all the jigsaw pieces together. But then realised he didn't know what the picture was he was trying to create. He didn't understand what was mystifying him. What was it that he was trying to understand? The more he thought, the more confused he became. But then, the more he thought, the clearer things became. None of this could he make sense of.

The Rabbi mused.

'Jesus, you are the Messiah.

Jesus, you are the Lord.

You became flesh and blood.

But how divine were you when you became like us?'

'Also, Jesus, what did your death achieve?

What did it accomplish?'

The Rabbi quoted words from the Psalms:

> *Your throne, O God, is forever and ever;*
> *the scepter of your kingdom is an upright*
> *scepter.*
>
> Psalm 45:6

'Are these verses really about you?' he asked into the darkness.

The Rabbi lay back and closed his eyes. He quickly drifted into sleep dreaming, thinking, debating.

Chapter Thirteen

The Rabbis last day of blindness

The Rabbi thanked the servant. The servant had helped the Rabbi move into the courtyard where he sat in the shade of the tree. When the Rabbi had been here before he wondered if the home had been built around this tree because it was so tall reaching to the roof and its branches extended the full length and width of the courtyard giving a lot of shade. He felt the cool breeze. He relaxed his shoulders. He heard the servant withdraw and wondered if he was seated the other side of the courtyard because he was always close by caring for him. The Rabbi was grateful for such small mercies. He had always taken such things for granted before. Reading, sight, life. He turned his mind to his future. What did Jesus want of him?

The Rabbi reflected on the events that had taken place so far. Before the servant had led him into the courtyard, he had had the usual string of visitors. The thought of having visitors made him feel like a patient. Judas, a few friends and his travelling companions had visited him wanting to find out how he was and if he needed anything. He hardly answered, which was what they had come to expect when they spoke to him. The Rabbi did wonder though about the servant. He had obviously not spoken a word about last night. And the servant, well there was something different about him this morning. What it was the Rabbi could not quite grasp. When he had helped the Rabbi into the courtyard it was as if, well, it was as if the servant had a gentleness, perhaps a respect about him that had not been there before. But it was not because of what the servant had said because he had not spoken any more than his usual few words.

The Rabbi sat back and thought about his dream. It was such a vivid dream. He could remember it clearly. He had had it again in the night but this time it was clearer. Someone had arrived at the home of Judas and had come to see him. He was called Ananias. Ananias was brought into the room where he was staying and introduced himself and then laid his hands on him and his eyes were healed. The dream was so real that when the Rabbi awoke, he had expected to see. Then he had realised it was only a dream. It was so clear and real. Who was this man called Ananias? There was no one in the house with that name to his knowledge. He said that Jesus had sent him. When had Jesus spoken with him? Ananias would come to heal him. He would come to fill him with the Holy Spirit of the Lord. He would come to baptise him in the name of Jesus. It was so real it was as if it had actually taken place. The Rabbi reflected, meditated and prayed. When would he come?

The Rabbi realised he was thinking of Jesus as his Lord. He wondered what this change would mean for him, in his life, in his career. Jesus was not just the

Lord, but his Lord. Jesus was not just the Messiah but his Messiah. These phrases were becoming familiar to him. No longer did they feel strange to think or speak them. No longer did he think of them blasphemous. He now saw them as truth. He knew he had changed. He sensed he was still changing. It was as if some hidden hand was quietly moulding him into...into what he did not know, but he knew something was happening. So much had changed in so little time. Barely a few days had passed since he had been met by his Lord on the road.

The Rabbi rested enjoying the sun on his face, warming him. The sun had moved across the sky and he was no longer in the cool of the shade. He did not ask the servant to move him but continued to sit, thinking and remembering. He wondered what his sister would think of his new-found knowledge.

Jesus, the Messiah.
Jesus, the son of God.

Jesus, our Messiah.

Jesus, our Lord.

He hoped that she would not reject him. He loved his sister and remembered the fun times they had had together as children when they were growing up. Their parents had treated them as equals in private but not in public. At home their father and also their mother had taught them both how to study, how to debate, but in the synagogue, and in the presence of the Rabbis who often visited their home, she was taught to be silent. Their father smiled and sometimes their mother despaired when he and his sister debated points of the law together. Their arguments were often heated, so heated she would end up first hitting him and then they would fight together. Even though she was now married, and had given birth to her first child, a boy, things had not changed. They still debated, discussed and argued. They did not fight, but his sister would still hit him. To her he was still the brother she loved, adored and looked up to.

He wanted to visit her and her family. He wanted to share what he had found, discovered, and reveal to them what he had been blind to. This thought, this hope excited him but also caused him sadness. What if she did not welcome him into her home? What if she did not share his passion for his Lord? He wiped tears away from his eyes. To die for Jesus, if that was his fate, he was beginning to accept that would happen. Now he had met Jesus...he was going to live his life for him...and if he died, well, at least he would be with his Lord for ever...but to live with his sister rejecting and scorning him...he did not want that to happen...he didn't think he could live if that did happen.

The Rabbi quietly prayed. 'Lord, I pray for my sister and her family. Open their hearts to my words about you when I testify to them about you. I want them to experience you in the way I have. I want them to choose you. I want them to see you as our Messiah and to behold your divinity.'

He prayed again, 'Lord, I don't want to be rejected by her, I don't want to lose my nephew. Open their minds, open their hearts. They need to be saved as I am saved.'

'Lord, it was if there was a veil over my mind and my heart as I read and studied your word before I met with you on the road. Thank you for removing that veil. I see things so clearly now in your word. I see the truth about who you are Jesus. I see how our Covenant is all about you. I ask Lord, for you to remove the veil from my sister. Remove that veil from my fellow countrymen. Remove that veil from my nation. Save them Lord, save them. They are all your chosen, precious people. The grace, the mercy, that you have poured out on me, pour out on them Lord.'

The Rabbi then spent what seemed like hours praying, interceding, for his sister, her family, his nation, his fellow Jews. He wanted them all to be saved. He didn't want anyone to miss out on what had been revealed to him. Jesus was both human and divine. Jesus was the Messiah. Jesus was the son of God. Jesus was Lord.

The Rabbi thought of the questions he had asked Jesus along with the many he had not yet voiced to him or found the words to express his questions. He hoped that he would get answers because he wanted to know. The Rabbi wanted to know the one he was now believing in. The Rabbi was not a man to have blind faith in God. He had studied. He had searched. He had wanted to know God. Now he wanted to know the son, Jesus, the son of God. The Rabbi smiled. He wanted Jesus to appear so he could discuss and debate with him as he did with his sister. He had so many questions. He thought of his sister. He chuckled to himself. The fighting, the arguing, the desire to be right. Jacob had wrestled with an angel. What if Jesus did appear again.... 'Well, You did say, Lord', the Rabbi said chuckling to himself:

Come now and let us reason together.
Isaiah 1:17

'But I promise, no fighting.'

The Rabbi knelt in prayer even though he was still in the Garden. He looked up with a soft look on his face and said,

'I give myself to you.

I dedicate myself to you.

I am here to serve you, to do your will, to establish your kingdom.

I will follow you wherever you lead me.

I lift all I am up to you. Use me for your Glory, for your kingdom.

I dedicate myself to you.

Use me for our Glory.

Keep me focused, pure, and ready for service.

May I not miss where you are leading, what you are saying, what you are asking.

Minister to me.

You own me.

I am yours.

Do what you need to do to me, so I am a worthy
vessel, ready for use.'

The Rabbi remained kneeling and lowered his head.

———————————————————

The Rabbi quietly said,

'O Lord God.

My God.

In you I trust.

I come under my prayer shawl, my tent of
meeting, to be before you, in your presence, to be still
before you, to hear your voice, to bless you, to
minister to you, to be blessed by the King of the
Universe, to be ministered to by my Shepherd, the
Shepherd of Israel, the Shepherd of my people and
my land.

I am here because I want fellowship with you.

Lord, I am here because

I seek your blessing

I want to be kept by you

I want your face to shine upon me

I want your grace, your compassion, your mercy

I want you to lift up your countenance upon me

I want your peace, your shalom

I want your name upon me

Amen, Lord.

Amen'

The Rabbi had been sitting quietly. He then without moving, gently said:

> *I know, O Lord, that Your judgments are right,*
> *and that You in faithfulness have afflicted me.*
> *Let Your merciful kindness comfort me,*
> *according to Your word to Your servant.*
> *Let Your compassion come to me, that I may live,*
> *for Your law is my delight.*
> Psalm 119:75-77

He then said:

"Let Your merciful kindness comfort me.
Let Your compassion come to me."

He gently repeated:

"Let Your merciful kindness comfort me.
Let Your compassion come to me."

He said:

"You in faithfulness have afflicted me."

He then asked,
'In faithfulness to whom, Lord?
In faithfulness to what?'

'In faithfulness to yourself and your covenant to your people?'

The Rabbi remembered what God had said to his forefather, Abraham:

"I will bless them who bless you
And curse him who curses you."

'Have I, by my actions, been cursing my own people, my own forefather?'

The Rabbi said, 'Have I been dishonouring my father...Abraham....is this why it has not gone well with me...is this why I am afflicted...? Is this why you blinded me?'

He then said:

Your hands have made me and fashioned me;
give me understanding, that I may learn Your
commandments.
Psalm 119:73

'I have ended up trying to steal, kill and destroy the very thing I love and lived for and wanted to protect. Is this why you punished me and blinded me?'

The Rabbi remembered the light, the voice and knelt in thanksgiving and worship.

'Lord,' he said, 'Thank you for your help. Thank you for revealing yourself to me. Thank you for being here with me. I kneel now before you to be with you. To hear from you. To listen, to learn. But I also just want to say, 'Thank you'. I trust you. I want to live life your way. I am yours. Use me for your Glory. Use me to do your will. Use me to build your kingdom. Show me what you want me to be and do for you. Show me where you want me to go to serve you.'

The Rabbi wanted to write and then remembered he was blind. He was beginning to feel frustrated. There was so much to remember, so much to think about, to pray about, to think through. He needed his eyes. He needed his pen. The Rabbi sensed something was about to happen but did not know what. He wanted to remember what was in his heart. It was important to him. He did not know what the future held and what he had gained he wanted to keep close to him.

He called for the servant and asked to be taken back to the room. Once seated he said to the servant, 'Write, please, write, quickly and carefully.'

The servant sat and the Rabbi began,

'I want to give victory and thanks to God, my Father.

To Jesus, my Saviour, my Lord, my King, my Saviour.

Victory and thanks to God, to Jesus, for the precious blood of Jesus, the Pascal Lamb or rather my Pascal Lamb.

Blood shed for me. Blood sealing a new covenant.

Victory and thanks for the precious blood that redeems me, protects me, saves me, washes me, cleanses me.

Victory and thanks because Father, you are my Rock. Victory because of Jesus, you are my Rock. Victory because you Holy Spirit counsel me, teach me, guide me. Victory because Jesus is an overcomer.

My Messiah overcame. My Messiah overcomes and I am an overcomer.'

The Rabbi sat silent. He finally said to the servant. 'Please give me what you have written'. He pushed the paper into one of his pockets. He thanked the servant.

The Rabbi smiled to himself. Pleased with what he had written. He felt somewhere at last. He felt ready, for something. He felt prepared for, whatever.

The servant left the room also smiling. Had he really heard the Rabbi say all that? The servant wished that he could have penned what the Rabbi had dictated to him. That was how he felt. One day he hoped to be able to thank the Rabbi.

Chapter Fourteen

The end had finally arrived for the Rabbi, no more waiting, but it really was not the end, just a new beginning.

It had been a long day. Ananias sat at his table to eat. He was alone, enjoying the peace and quiet of his room. He could hear the noise of the children playing, the parents talking. He took the bread and broke it.

He blessed it saying, 'Blessed are you, Lord our God, Ruler of the universe who brings forth bread from the earth.'

He then said, 'Lord Jesus, My King, My Messiah, I remember you as I eat this bread. I remember you are with me. I remember what you have done for me.'

Ananias paused, he sensed he was not alone. He heard a footstep behind him. He turned— 'My Lord!'.

Jesus stood looking at him. Jesus then spoke with him about the Rabbi. He explained how the Rabbi in the House of Judas was to take his name to all those not living in the Promised Land. To fellow Jews and also to the nations. He explained how the Rabbi was to proclaim his name before rulers, before those who many of his followers would never be able to reach, even to Caesar.

Ananias sat there listening, still holding the broken bread as if he was frozen in time.

And then came the words from Jesus that caused Ananias to flinch. Jesus explained how he wanted Ananias to go to Judas's home and meet the Rabbi. Ananias was to bring healing to his eyes and baptise him.

Ananias moved and spoke for the first time. 'But Lord, I have heard about this man. How he has harmed your people. He is here to arrest your followers who are here. He is here to arrest your people in this house. He is here for me.'

Jesus quietly explained that the Rabbi was expecting him, waiting for his visit, praying for him to arrive. All would be well, Jesus assured him. Jesus explained how he had shown the Rabbi in a vision how he was to lay hands on him and bring healing to him. Then Jesus told Ananias many other things about what the Rabbi would do, how he would serve Him.

And then, just as quickly and quietly as he had appeared, Jesus disappeared.

Ananias sat there. Not daring to move. Not wanting to move. Not wanting to lose this precious moment. Then he dropped the bread, left his meal and hurried to meet this Rabbi.

There was a knock at the door. The servant remained near the Rabbi but listened. It was too late for callers wanting to meet with Judas. He listened and heard the voice of Ananias. The servant rushed to the door and intervened. He said that he would escort the visitor to the Rabbi's room. As the servant led the way he whispered to Ananias, wanting to know why he was here and what he wanted to meet the Rabbi for? He received no reply other than a signal to remain silent.

Ananias stood at the door and looked at the Rabbi. He took a deep breath, walked across the room, laid his hands on the eyes of the blind Rabbi and said:

> Brother Saul, the Lord Jesus, who appeared to you on the way as you came, has sent me so that you may see again and be filled with the Holy Spirit.
> Acts 9:17

Ananias laid his hands over the Rabbi's eyes.

The Rabbi regained his sight.

Ananias did not wait for a response from the Rabbi but quietly continued and said:

> *The God of our fathers has appointed you to know His will and to see the Just One and to hear His voice, for you will be His witness to all men of what you have seen and heard. And now why do you wait? Rise, be baptized and wash away your sins, and call on the name of the Lord.*
> Acts 22:14

Ananias baptised Saul using the water in the jug that had remained untouched by the Rabbi.

The servant smiled to himself. *"Brother Saul"* Ananias had said. The Rabbi was now his brother in Christ.

Ananias spoke quietly and quickly to the Rabbi and then left the room. He kept his head bowed, not even looking at the servant. It was as if he wanted to be invisible, as if he didn't want anyone to know he had been in the house. He was known by all in the city as the local leader of those who had chosen to believe and follow Jesus of Nazareth as the Messiah. He had been a follower since the beginning along with the apostles, but this was not a place where he was welcome, nor did he want to be found, even though he attended the synagogue that Judas was a part of.

Ananias left quickly and quietly but his presence did not go unnoticed. As soon as Ananias left, Judas arrived. He entered the room and shut the door. The servant didn't hear anything. The door was shut. He strained to listen but could only make out the voices of the two Rabbis but could not make hear any words. But then the voice of Judas was raised. It was as if Judas was trying to restrain and control himself whilst the Rabbi was in total control.

Time passed and then he heard his master raise his voice again. 'Unless you repent of this madness', he said, 'you will not be welcome in my home again. Have you lost your senses!' Judas stormed out.

The servant stood with his head bowed and just said, 'Master' as he passed to acknowledge Judas.

He watched as the Rabbi walked over to the table and poured himself water to drink. There was not much water left in the jug after Ananias had poured it over the Rabbi. He turned to look at the servant and asked him if he would get him some food and more water plus a little wine. His hair still dripping. His shoulders and the top of his tunic still wet.

The servant stood and watched the Rabbi. He didn't realise that he was staring. There was something different about the Rabbi. He had an authority about him that he had never seen before. He had a confidence as well. A confidence that showed something the servant could not quite explain...he was now in control...? The servant was not sure what it was, but he sensed there was something new, something special, something bestowed upon him by the Holy Spirit. The Rabbi looked at him. 'Well, what are you waiting for?' 'I could starve to death whilst you stand there gawping', the Rabbi said trying to conceal a smile.

The servant unaware that he had been staring, apologised, and turned away quickly. As he went to the kitchens, he smiled to himself. Life would be very different now he thought.

The Rabbi quietly ate alone. But he knew he was not alone. His Lord was with him. After he had eaten, he dismissed the servant. Let him sleep in his own bed tonight. How many nights had he faithfully been watching, waiting, ready to serve? The Rabbi was grateful.

The Rabbi rose from his seat, lifted his eyes and arms in worship.

'O, God, King of the Universe.
Jesus, son of God, King of Israel.
Jesus, King of God's Kingdom.
Rule over me.
I choose your rule for my life.
I want you to rule and reign over me.'

The Rabbi knelt in prayer, covered himself with his prayer shawl and said,

'Father, thank you for all that you have revealed to me in the last few days, for all you have shown me, taught me. Thank you for what you have done for me. Forgiven me. Cleansed me. Purified me.'

'Jesus, son of God, Lord of my life, thank you that you revealed yourself to me on the road here. You have changed me. You have—well—overwhelmed me. My world has changed but I don't want to lose what you have given me, blessed me with. I don't want to go back to how I was.'

'Jesus, I want to know you. I want to hear from you. I want to have fellowship with you. I have found you. I want more of you.'

'Father, I thought I had reached the depths with you but now I know I did not really know you as I thought I did, as I want to. I want more of you, Father.

Please keep purifying me. Refining me. Helping me.

Open my eyes. I don't want to be misled again. I don't want to cause you pain ever again.'

The Rabbi was seated in the chair. He had been thinking about whom He had met on the road. The Lord. Jesus. The Lord Jesus. The son of God. The Messiah. The true King of Israel. The meeting had been so real, it was not something he had imagined. He knew it was real. He knew He had met Jesus. He knew Jesus had spoken to him. But, in some way it all seemed a dream. Not real.

The Rabbi spoke quietly,

'Lord Jesus, please keep revealing yourself to me. Please keep guiding me, teaching me, meeting with me. I love your presence, your peace. I want a greater knowledge of you, your words, your teachings. I want a greater intimacy with you and your presence. I don't know what is going to happen. But I don't want to ever lose what I have gained. Take me deeper into you. Protect me from the world.'

The Rabbi fell quiet.

He stared, as if He was looking at someone.

The Rabbi stood. Bowed his head. He said,

'Father, Lord, God...

"Holy, holy, holy

Lord God Almighty,

Who was, and is, and is to come.'

He continued,

'Father, thank you that your son shed his precious blood for me. his blood brings me forgiveness, cleansing, restoration. It removes all my regrets, all my shame. Sprinkle me afresh in your blood. I feel unworthy, guilty, worthless - cleanse me, clean me afresh. Now you have saved me I see the enormity of my sin, my errors, my failings. The way I hurt you whilst seeking to honour you. Father, forgive me. I condemned your son, the one you sent to save me.'

The Rabbi said:

Create in me a clean heart, O God,
and renew a right spirit within me.
Do not cast me away from Your presence,
and do not take Your Holy Spirit from me.
Restore to me the joy of Your salvation,
and uphold me with Your willing spirit.

Psalm 51:10-12

I, who claimed to be your friend.

I, who claimed to be so loyal and faithful to you would have crucified your son as I imprisoned and killed his followers.

The Rabbi felt the tears rolling down his cheeks.

Tears from knowing he was experiencing something he had no right to enjoy, the joy of salvation.

He muttered, 'Thank you, thank you, thank you.'

The Rabbi stood, prayer shawl around his shoulders, with arms outstretched to heaven. He recited the opening verses of a Psalm:

> *Blessed is he*
> *whose transgression is forgiven,*
> *whose sin is covered.*
> *Blessed is the man*
> *against whom the Lord does not count iniquity,*
> *and in whose spirit there is no deceit.*
> Psalm 31:1-2

The Rabbi began to think about the visit from Ananias, what he had said, what he had done. The Lord had kept his word, he was able to see again. He knew that he would never take his sight for granted again. He walked over to the table and touched the scrolls and parchments. He looked at the words. He was able to see and read. He felt so grateful and praised God for his sight. He thanked God for the faithfulness and obedience of Ananias.

The Rabbi reflected on how he had been baptized. Such a simple ceremony as it should be, but the effect. The Rabbi smiled in amazement. He had never been filled with God's Spirit before. He was overwhelmed by the experience. And also, being able to pray in the language the Holy Spirit filled him with. Was it the language of heaven? The language of angels? The language of divine mysteries?

The Rabbi had quickly learned early in his life that anything that helps you pray and get closer to God can quickly become a dead work. He wondered if this would ever happen with this new language. Already the Rabbi was thinking ahead. Many followers of Jesus were blessed and grateful to be full of the God's Holy Spirit. They lived in the now. Not so with the Rabbi. He was already thinking of the future. Already his mind was filling with questions, seeking answers. Can I now pray without ceasing? How do I always live listening to the voice of the Holy Spirit? Could life now be like a journey where we travel and walk together? Keeping step with each other or rather me keeping step with Him? Zeal was rising up once again to consume him.

The Rabbi then remembered how his friend Judas had spoken to him. What Judas had said. The Rabbi knew Judas. Judas was not a man who spoke hastily. What he said, he meant. When he made threats, he carried them out.

'Lord' the Rabbi began to pray. Then he stopped and sat down. Tears began to fall down his cheeks. This time, not tears of joy but of shame and repentance. The Rabbi said, 'Lord I was going to pray to you and say:

Be my rock of refuge
to enter continually;
You have given commandment to save me;
for You are my rock and my stronghold.
Deliver me, O my God, out of the hand of the
wicked,
out of the hand of the unjust and cruel man.
Psalm 71:3-4

I know Judas is my friend, but I also know what he believes and the opinion he holds about those who believe Jesus is your son and the Messiah. Unless I deny you then he has threatened to be unjust and cruel towards me. As I was going to pray to you and to ask that you would protect me from him...I realised that to the followers of Jesus...I was also the unjust, the cruel, the wicked man. Many begged me for mercy. I ignored their pleas. Lord, can you ever forgive me? I was unjust, cruel and wicked to my fellow countrymen. I refused mercy when it was within my power to give mercy. Can you find it in your heart to forgive me for being so unjust, so cruel?'

'Lord, I will not deny you. I will not ask for mercy from Judas. I will not ask you to protect me from what I deserve.'

The Rabbi held his prayer shawl in his hands and lifted it up to heaven. It was as if he was presenting the Lord with a gift, the gift of his prayer shawl.

The Rabbi said,

'Thank you for this prayer shawl.
I offer it to you as a symbol of giving my life to you.
Thank you that I am able to come and meet with you.
Thank you that I am able to have fellowship with you.
Thank you that I can share with you.
Thank you for your help in the last few days.
I can see you helping, strengthening, guiding me.
Thank you.

I come here to be in your presence, to fellowship
with you.
You are my God.
My Rock.
My Peace.
Thank you.
You are my God, my Rock, my peace'.

The Rabbi stood, raised his arms, lifted his eyes to
heaven and said:

> *O afflicted one, tossed with tempest and not*
> *comforted,*
> *I will lay your stones with fair colors*
> *and lay your foundations with sapphires.*
> *I will make your windows of agates,*
> *and your gates of crystal,*
> *and all your borders of precious stones.*
> *All your sons shall be taught of the Lord,*
> *and great shall be the peace of your sons.*
> *In righteousness you shall be established;*

you shall be far from oppression,

for you shall not fear,

and from terror,

for it shall not come near you.

Indeed they shall surely assail you fiercely, but

not from Me.

Whoever assails you shall fall for your sake.

Isaiah 54:11-15

'Lord, you prophesied about us as a nation, a people, a city and said that you would rebuild us. You have been faithful to your word. I need you to do these things to me. If I am to serve you, I need you to prepare me. All my life I have been preparing myself for my future. I need, I want, I desire to put all that behind me and be the man you now need me to be to serve you, to honour you, to bring Glory to your name. I need to be all of you and nothing of me. I have been established in my own righteousness. Now I need to be established in your righteousness. Thank you, Lord, thank you.'

The Rabbi slept soundly for the remainder of that night.

Chapter Fifteen

Just before dawn the next day

The servant was ready to leave the house early next morning as he often did before any one was up. He turned the corner to go towards the door leading into the street when he bumped into Judas, 'Master, I apologise, I did not know you were up. Is there anything I can get for you?'

Normally Judas was never around until later. Why now? Judas ignored him. The servant hung back waiting, what was happening? He heard voices and footsteps. Judas spoke in a low, stern voice. It was as if he was struggling to keep his emotions under control. He was speaking to someone the servant could not see. He then heard Judas say, 'If you leave this house now, without giving up this madness, you are not to return and never to come here again.'

'I am sorry Judas, but I must', said the Rabbi and then the servant saw the Rabbi walk towards the door and leave. The servant noticed that the Rabbi did not have his bag with him, so he slipped quickly back into his room to collect it. He saw several other documents on the table. He just picked them all up and stuffed them into the bag. He slipped out of the house unnoticed. He ran down the street. 'Rabbi, you forgot your bag.' The servant did not give it to the Rabbi but carried it for him walking next to him. The Rabbi walked quietly next to the servant, allowing the servant to lead the way. Both preoccupied with their own thoughts and prayers.

Ananias was welcoming guests into his home. It was still dark. Dawn was not far away. The day light would soon come, and the hustle and bustle of

217

another day would begin. But these meetings and these guests were so precious to him. They were fellow believers in Jesus who was their Lord, their Messiah, the son of God. They gathered together to break bread, to pray and to remember Jesus. Then they would all as quickly and as quietly as they had appeared at his door, disappear to start their day.

They were all gathered as Ananias welcomed them. It had not gone unnoticed that one of their fellowship was missing. He was not known for being late. The door opened and Ananias smiled at the late comer and his guest. The servant smiled back and with amusement looked at the faces of the believers as they stared at his guest. They knew it was rude to stare and point, but they couldn't stop themselves.

The servant sat down and beckoned his guest, his new brother in the Messiah to sit next to him. The Rabbi smiled awkwardly and sat down.

For several days Saul was with the disciples in Damascus. Immediately he preached in the synagogues that the Christ is the son of God. All who heard him were amazed and said, "Is not this he who killed those who called on this name in Jerusalem, and came here with that intent, to bring them bound to the chief priests?" Yet Saul increased all the more with power and confounded the Jews living in Damascus, proving that this One is the Christ.

After many days had passed, the Jews arranged to kill him. But their scheme was known by Saul. They watched the gates day and night to kill him. But the disciples took him by night, and lowered him in a basket through the wall.

Acts 9:19-24

After leaving the house of Judas the Rabbi had stayed with Ananias. 'What is one more refugee?' thought Ananias. The Rabbi became a member of his flock, his church.

Ananias and the servant were chosen to help the Rabbi leave the city. Everyone wanted to help, to see him on his way but it only needed a few people. They made their way through the city. The servant quickly and confidently led Ananias and the Rabbi through narrow dark passageways to a deserted part of the wall. Ananias wanted to bless his newest disciple as he fled. As they were beginning to lower the Rabbi over the wall the servant said, 'Master, you will need this', and passed him his bag. The servant thought that the Rabbi needed a good servant to look after him. As the Rabbi was lowered, he looked at the servant, he still did not know his name. 'Ananias, look after him. He is precious. He has been very good to me. I hope we can meet again.' The Rabbi then disappeared down the wall, in the basket, into the darkness.

Chapter Sixteen

The new beginning.

The Rabbi did share his new found belief in Jesus with his sister and she did not reject him nor his Messiah. Her family embraced Jesus as the Messiah and the son of God. The Rabbi's nephew later saved his life as had Ananias and the servant.

The Rabbi did stand before Caesar.

The Rabbi also died for his faith in Jesus, but this did not happen in the following days as he had expected and was prepared for. That day came about thirty years later. His prayer was answered—it was by the sword.

Did the Rabbi meet the servant again? Well, that's another story.

Day by Day: Healing Scriptures
by Lindsay Hassall
ISBN: 978-0-9932090-9-3
78 pages
Paperback

Praying for Israel and the Jewish people in the last days
by Lindsay Hassall
ISBN: 978-1-9997224-6-3
89 pages
Paperback

Day by Day with the Bread and the Cup
by Lindsay Hassall
ISBN: 978-1-8381828-1-6
109 pages
Paperback

www.GileadBooksPublishing.com

BV - #0078 - 180322 - C0 - 203/127/13 - PB - 9781838182823 - Gloss Lamination